Tom Clancy's
Net Force Explorers:
Safe House

Created by Tom Clancy and Steve Pieczenik

HEADLINE BOOK PUBLISHING
a division of the Hodder Headline Group
338 Euston Road
LONDON NW1

HEADLINE
FEATURE

First published in 2000
by HEADLINE BOOK PUBLISHING

A HEADLINE FEATURE paperback

10 9 8 7 6 5 4 3 2 1

ISBN 0 7472 6175 X

Typeset by
Letterpart Limited, Reigate, Surrey

Printed and bound in Great Britain by
Mackays of Chatham plc, Chatham, Kent

HEADLINE BOOK PUBLISHING
A divi

Acknowledgements

We'd like to thank the following people, without whom this book would have not been possible: Diane Duane, for help in rounding out the manuscript; Martin H. Greenberg, Larry Segriff, Denise Little, and John Helfers at Tekno Books; Mitchell Rubenstein and Laurie Silvers at BIG Entertainment; Tom Colgan of Penguin Putnam Inc.; Robert Youdelman, Esquire; and Tom Mallon, Esquire; and Robert Gottlieb of the William Morris Agency, agent and friend. We much appreciated the help.

Prologue

His father had told him repeatedly that everything would be all right. The two things that surprised Laurent, after the fact, were how little he believed this – even though he went along with the plan – and, even though he'd been told there was nothing to be afraid of, how blindingly afraid he was.

The talk between him and his pop had been very light all the way to the train station – chatter about school, and school food, and Laurent's performance in the last soccer game against Garoafa (it had been terrible – Laurent wished his father wouldn't keep bringing it up).

They had walked as usual from the side street where their apartment was located, into the middle of town through Piata Unirii with its huge, ugly, blockish high-rise buildings left over from the middle of the last century, and out the other side of the plaza to the Focsani train station. There they made their way past the armed guards as usual, showing their ID cards and their train passes, and went down the stairs under the tracks, coming up on the other side to stand on the bleak gray platform with all the other people in their dark coats and somber dresses. The weather was unseasonably chilly – a surprisingly raw wind for June was sweeping down from the low misty line of the mountains to the north. The wind whistled in the overhead wires that powered the local electric trains – the few of them still running – and made Laurent shiver. At least that was the excuse he gave himself.

From down the tracks came a loud, sour hoot, the cry of one of the old diesel locomotives usually used for hauling freight, but now released for passenger-hauling work in the summer, when there was theoretically no need to supply the carriages with heat. Laurent was a little train-mad, as were many kids in his part of the world. The trains spoke to them of travel, of other places different from home, and of (whisper it) freedom – places where (rumor had it) the transit went on one rail rather than two, on maglev rather than wheels, or hybrid air/lox jets rather than turboprops.

There was no way to tell if the rumors were true – the government didn't let the local Net or media say much about such things, all products of the decadent cultures outside the borders. But in the meantime, the trains Laurent could see any day at the station were interesting, if not particularly varied, and he knew them all like old friends. This one was ST43-260, a diesel made at the old 23 August Factory down in Bucuresti, a low, flat-faced locomotive with two headlamps and big windshield plates that made it look like a huge, dim, friendly bug. Lurching and creaking, with the ting and clang of hanging 'tween-cars chains accompanying it as it came, the dirty cream and dingy red ST43 pulled up to them and past them, hauling the ten second-class carriages, all ancient CFR stock from before the turn of the century, creaking and groaning behind it. It came grumbling and hissing to a stop, the diesel roar of the loco only slightly subdued by a couple of hundred yards' distance.

Normally they would have gotten right on – other people started pushing past them and doing so. But his father was facing down the platform, looking for someone, and Laurent found himself suddenly wishing, irrationally, *Don't let him come. Let's not do it. I wish—*

'There he is,' his father said, suddenly sounding very relieved. 'Iolae!' He waved at a broad figure in a dark coat, away down the platform.

The figure approached them, hurrying a little through the crowd, smiling, and as he came up to them and put out a hand for Laurent's father to shake, Laurent was filled with misgivings. The two men didn't look anything like brothers, his father tall and blond and a little hawkish-looking, except for the glasses, which transformed the hawk-face into the slight squinting expression of an owl; the newcomer shorter, stouter, broad-faced, balding. *This isn't going to fool anybody,* Laurent thought, the sweat breaking out on him. *And when the police figure it out, they'll just take us off the train and—*

'Thought I was going to be late, didn't you?' said his 'uncle,' and bent to hug Laurent. Laurent reciprocated, but there was no warmth about it, though neither his father nor his 'uncle' seemed to notice.

They pushed their way into the line with all the other people, and got up into the train, showing their ID cards and tickets again to the bored guard standing in the doorway beside the train conductor. Then they slowly made their way down the aisle, Laurent glancing around him as he always did in hopes of spotting a piece of new, or at least different, equipment on this line. *Not much chance of that, though,* he thought. He knew this train-car by heart – the grimy linoleum – Laurent sometimes spent long minutes trying to figure out what pattern had been there when the linoleum was new – no telling now – the torn or cracked maroon 'leather' seats, cream-enameled walls with the paint chipping, bent-out-of-shape wire mesh luggage racks propped up high between back-to-back pairs of seats. Laurent sometimes tried to imagine what this stock had looked like when it was new, back in 1980 sometime. It was like trying to imagine what dinosaurs had looked like. He sighed and followed his father and 'uncle' until his pop saw an open seat, and they all crowded together onto it.

All the while the newcomer and Laurent's father were talking as if they actually were brothers, laughing sometimes, talking about work. Mostly this meant Laurent's father not saying much, of course. You never knew who might be listening. He was a biologist, but he rarely spoke much about exactly what kind of biology he was doing, and wise people didn't ask. It was just as well, since he was working for the government. With the privilege came a certain amount of responsibility – or, to Laurent's mind, a certain amount of danger. But he didn't mention this any more than his father did. It was understood.

After a few moments the train lurched forward, and Laurent sighed a little, relieved, and not entirely certain why. Normally his father would get off at the next stop, and then Laurent would get off at the one after that, closest to his school, which was just outside the Focsani town limits. Today, though, was special. Today he was going on a day trip with his Uncle Iolae to Brasov, to see the old castle where Voivod Vlad Dracul had lived, across the border in Transylvania. He had repeated the story over to himself a hundred times since his father first explained it to him, doing his best to learn it so well that it would sound natural if somebody from the police asked him—

And the train was stopping already at Focsani-Nov. Laurent gulped. His father glanced at him. 'So enjoy yourself,' his father said, reached out, and gave Laurent a hug.

4

Laurent hugged him back – and suddenly felt terrible pain all through him, and sweat starting out again all over him, so that he was *sure* everyone must be able to see it. This was it, they were saying goodbye, and he didn't know when he was going to see his father again. *I might never—* But no. That was a dumb idea. No matter how dangerous things were getting at work, his father wouldn't send him away forever without telling him first.

Would he?

His father pushed him away, not hard, but briskly enough, as if they both had things to be doing. 'You mind your uncle now,' he said, and patted Laurent on the shoulder. 'Have a nice day.'

'I will, Pop,' he said, his mouth dry. Laurent's father reached down to the other man, shook his hand again warmly, if casually, the gesture of someone he expected to see again that afternoon – except that Laurent knew he wouldn't. And for the first time Laurent began to realize that his father was a pretty good actor, and that could be one of the reasons that all this *would* work out the way he said it would.

'You have a nice time now,' his pop said to 'Uncle Iolae.' 'Thanks for taking him. Don't let him get out of hand.'

'I don't imagine he will,' said the other man. He thumped Laurent's father good-naturedly on the arm, and Laurent turned to watch Dr Armin Darenko walk away, hidden after only a moment or two by other people getting off the train.

He gulped again, and tried to get some control over himself, tried to look normal. 'How long will it take us to get there?' he asked his 'uncle.'

'Uncle Iolae' looked at his watch. 'About three hours. Half an hour to the border, then checks and a change of

5

trains . . . after that, fifty minutes to Ploiesti . . . then another two hours to Brasov.'

Laurent nodded, looked out the window . . . and found his father looking in at him. The face he saw there was one holding itself calm, but Laurent knew his father well enough that the attempt to hide the emotion didn't work. Laurent did his best to hold his own worry inside as tightly as he could, for there was no point in burdening his father with it. He smiled and waved, and his father smiled, too, just a crack of smile, a thin, strained look. And then Dr Darenko turned and left.

Laurent could have wept at the suddenness of it, at the way the pain and uncertainty stabbed him . . . except that would have given everything away. He said nothing, and the train started up again, pulling forward with a groan. Then his 'uncle' looked at him and said softly, 'I know.'

Nothing more.

But there was something bracing about it – the sense of a shared secret, and someone who understood. And shared danger, that was there, too, so that Laurent reminded himself that he needed to get a grip. He got a grip, straightened himself in the seat, blinked, and then sneezed on purpose so as to get rid of the threatening burning in his eyes.

The next hour was nerve-wracking in a way Laurent hadn't expected. Until his father had left him with this stranger, it had all seemed like a game – exciting, not real. But now it was real. He was leaving, for who knew how long, and he might not see any of this familiar terrain again for a long time . . . maybe even never. He looked out the window and stared, when the train stopped again, at the band of trees that hid his school from the little station and the train tracks. All the kids he knew there, the ones he liked . . . he might never see them again. *Then again,* he thought, *the ones I don't like, I might never see* them *again either* . . . But this was less of a consolation than he expected it to be, and as the train pulled away, he found himself staring at everything they passed – trees, patches of gravel by the tracks, old factories, junked cars – as if trying to imprint them on his brain, to memorize them. *I may never pass this way again* . . .

Soon enough they pulled into the town and station of Sihlea, where they would have to change trains, and Laurent and his 'uncle' got up and made their way off, slowly, behind everyone else. This was new territory to Laurent, since it was illegal for 'citizens not yet of age' to travel more than ten miles from home without a citizen-of-age to accompany them. His father rarely had time to take him anywhere, since the government kept him busy all the time in the labs and offices in Focsani and Adjud.

Laurent had sometimes grumbled about this. If his pop was doing such important services for the state, whatever it was he was doing, then why didn't they let him get some rest sometimes, so that he would do the work even better? But having seen the look on his father's face the first time he voiced this opinion out loud at home, Laurent now kept such ideas to himself. He might be thirteen, but he wasn't stupid. Everyone at school knew there were subjects in their country that could cause you, if you were heard bringing them up, to be arrested and tried . . . or worse, simply to vanish and never be seen again. Whispered opinion varied wildly on whether these were good or bad ideas. What no one argued about was that it was bad to vanish.

As they got off, Laurent glanced around him. The platform was small, too small to take two trains front to back, so as the one they had been on pulled away, the second one pulled up to the platform from where it had been waiting in the nearby marshaling yard. Laurent's 'uncle' took him amiably by the arm, and the two of them joined the line of people waiting to get into the nearest door of the train.

It was identical to the first one as to grime and age, though slightly interesting to Laurent because he hadn't seen this particular car working this line before. When the train started up again, he looked out the window at the new and unfamiliar countryside outside the town until his 'uncle' said, 'Here comes the conductor. Give me your papers.' Laurent reached into his pocket and handed them over. He tended to watch his paperwork carefully, as most people did in a country where being caught without it could get you sent to jail, so, never having taken his eyes off what he gave his 'uncle,' he was astonished when the conductor came up to them, checked the papers, punched their tickets, and Laurent took his papers back . . . and found they were not the ones he had given his uncle.

He forced himself not to stare or look surprised. But Laurent was as annoyed as someone who'd just had a magician pull an egg out of his ear and didn't understand how it had been done. He glanced at his ID card, his 'internal passport,' and saw that his name was now Nicolae Arnui, as his father had told him it would be. The picture was his own. The embossing and the hologram looked exactly as they should have, a little beat-up. Laurent started wondering how much his father had had to pay for this forgery – and the sweat broke out on him yet again. Forging ID was one of the offenses for which, if they caught you, they shot you. And being caught carrying the forged ID could make you vanish . . .

'So tell me about that game with Garoafa,' his 'uncle' said. Laurent groaned but, playing along, he told him all about it . . . while thinking how strange it was, all of a sudden, to have an uncle. Well, he *had* had one, but that uncle, the real Uncle Iolae, had been trapped on the Transylvanian side of the border when Partition happened, and when he tried to come back home, he vanished. No one in the family had talked about it except his mother. Now that she was gone, no one talked about it at all.

This new Uncle Iolae reminded Laurent strangely of his father, in the way that, when they weren't talking, he would sit quiet for long minutes at a time, looking out at the landscape as if memorizing it. His father had that thinking, memorizing look no matter what he looked at, so that when he returned to paying attention to you after a spell of it, the absolute immediacy of his regard came as a surprise. He might be a dreamer, but he was one of the kind who upon waking immediately went about the business of building what he'd seen in his dreams. Laurent had slowly started to understand that people like this are both valuable and dangerous – dangerous both to themselves and to those around them. It was why the government made sure his pop had a good apartment and access to the 'special purchases' parts of the state grocery and hardware collective stores, and why Laurent had new school uniforms every year, and went to a school that had better books and computers than any other in the city, and his father didn't have to pay extra for it. But at the same time, there was always the hint that, if the dreams stopped, and the building of what was in them stopped, then all this would stop as well. There were other prices to pay, too – the knowledge that they were often watched, both of them, but his father most carefully of all. His father didn't mention it, but there were times at home when Laurent could feel the fear more clearly than usual, the sense of being watched and obscurely threatened. And lately the fear had become stronger and stronger . . . until finally his father had told him, two days ago, that they were getting out. Or, rather, that Laurent was.

'Here we are,' said his 'uncle,' and Laurent looked up in shock to see that they had reached Rinnicu Sanat, the town at the border. *The border.* A thrill of fear went through him. If the guards realized that the ID was fake—

He breathed in and out and tried once again to calm himself as he got up and followed his 'uncle' down the aisle of the train. They got out into a slightly warmer day than the one they had left behind in Focsani. This area had some hills between it and the mountains, Laurent remembered from school, so that it had a more sheltered 'microclimate.' But he was still having to fight off the shivers.

Come on, he told himself. *If you look nervous, and give it away, they'll come after Pop—*

His 'uncle' led him down to the end of the platform, down a flight of stairs, through a dark tunnel under the tracks, and up the far side, using another flight of stairs, to a middle platform in the station. There was another train waiting, an unfamiliar one, and between them and it, at a guardpost mounted at the top of the stairs and fenced in with wire, were guards with machine guns . . . and the police.

He saw just one ISF man in his neat gray uniform, watching them come up the steps. But one was enough. And the two soldiers who stood there watching them come up the stairs looked like they hated the day, and hated standing there, and would hate Laurent, too, if he gave them the slightest excuse – a word or a look, anything that would draw their attention away from how much they were hating everything else.

This was the last barrier. Laurent hardly dared to look

up as he brought out his ID card and his train ticket and handed them to the ISF man, afraid that he would notice that they were damp from Laurent's sweating hands. The policeman stuck the card in the reader, and turned his attention to the ticket as the reader beeped softly to itself. 'A lot of counterfeits coming through lately,' he said absently, scratching the paper of the ticket.

Laurent stood there frozen.

'What some people won't do,' his 'uncle' said calmly, holding out his own ticket and card.

The reader stopped beeping, and the ISF man took out Laurent's card, read it carefully, and handed it back to him. 'Why aren't you in school?' he said.

'Cultural holiday,' said Laurent, and the dryness of his mouth suddenly strangled him, making it impossible to get out the casual-sounding response he had been rehearsing for the past three days.

'Vlad Dracul's old castle,' said his 'uncle,' as the ISF man shoved his card in turn into the reader. 'I went to see it when I was his age.'

'Ugly old pile of rocks,' said the ISF man, not impressed. 'And the capitalist bloodsuckers actually charge you money to see it. Waste of time.' He pulled Laurent's 'uncle's' card out of the reader, handed it back. 'Still, a nice summer day . . . any excuse to get out of school, huh?'

Laurent found his attention fixed irrationally on the barrel of the gun belonging to the soldier standing closest to him. It seemed the ugliest thing he had ever seen.

'I *like* school,' he said abruptly. Though not entirely true, this was at least an entire sentence, and could be taken as a suggestion that he wasn't frightened out of his wits.

The soldier holding the gun laughed. 'Don't worry, we won't report you for wanting to be elsewhere,' he said,

11

and glanced at the ISF man, who gave the two of them one last look.

'Go on,' the policeman said. 'Have a nice day with the old bloodsucker. No fraternizing with the western tourists, now.'

'Don't care to talk to them much anyway,' said his 'uncle' righteously. 'Dirty profiteering foreigners. Come on, Niki.'

They walked on through the chainlink-fence gate, toward the train waiting on the platform. Then, 'Nicolae!' someone shouted behind them.

The sound of the shout was as sudden and startling as a gunshot. Laurent turned, looked back to see who was getting yelled at – then belatedly realized it was him. The ISF man, expressionless, watching them, turned away. The soldier laughed, waved them on again.

They turned again, walked another twenty or thirty yards down the platform and climbed on the waiting train.

'Ha ha,' Laurent muttered under his breath as they got up into it and turned right through the narrow door into the second-class carriage. 'Big joke, very funny.'

'Maybe,' his 'uncle' said softly. Laurent swallowed.

They got into the carriage, sat down and waited. The carriage was very quiet. People came and settled down around them, waiting in bored silence. Down the carriage, a frustrated fly bumped against the windows, trying to get out – bumped, buzzed, bumped again. Laurent watched the soldiers and ISF men going up the length of the train, shutting the doors that still lay open. *Bang! Bang! Bang!* The sound, in this nervous silence, was too much like gunfire for Laurent's liking. The ISF man who had looked at him now came down the length of the train again, peering in the windows. Laurent made it his business to be looking out the other side of the train when the man came by again, paused outside the window, then passed on.

Silence again. Laurent sat and twitched.

Then there came a *crash!* From down the locomotive end of the train, and the world lurched forward as the diesel's sudden convulsive pull reverberated through the cars of the train. They were moving.

The train accelerated to about fifty km/h and held that speed for maybe twenty minutes. With the unfriendly eyes outside the window gone now, Laurent pressed his nose to the smudged, dusty glass and looked hungrily out at the world. It streamed by him – houses with untidy gardens and houses with tidy ones, cabbage patches and corn piled up in broad fields already cut to stubble, parking lots, level crossings, manufacturing collectives with oil sumps built into the concrete 'back yards,' piles of old tires, chained-up, ratty-looking guard dogs yapping inanely at the passing train. Then suddenly the locomotive began to slow again, and Laurent realized that they were coming to another fence, one which came right up to the edges of the track. Slowly the train lumbered through, past more guards on a concrete platform, the guards looking at the train with weary or even hostile eyes.

Then they were on the other side of the fence, and there were guards there, too, equally weary-looking, but the uniforms were different, blue instead of gray. The train rumbled past them all, left them behind.

Laurent's heart leapt irrationally. He looked over at his 'uncle,' who was gazing out the other side of the train, past two dark-dressed ladies with parcels in their laps. After a moment, as if he felt Laurent's glance, he looked over at him. He didn't manage an answering smile, but he raised his eyebrows.

'Was that it?' Laurent said.

A slight nod. Then his 'uncle' leaned back. 'A while yet before Brasov,' he said. 'I'm going to take a nap.'

'Okay,' Laurent said. His 'uncle' shrugged his jacket up into a more comfortable conformation around him, closed his eyes. Laurent, turning to stare out the window, found that everything suddenly looked different. This was the beginning of the rest of the world.

After that, everything seemed to happen very fast. He was not able to burn the landscape into his mind as he had been before the border. There was too much of it, too many new things – first the mountains, then the broad plain beyond them. And he started seeing things he had never seen before, but had only heard about. They got off at Brasov and changed trains, and to Laurent's amazement no one even bothered to check anything but their tickets. Also, waiting for them at the next platform was, not just one more weary turn-of-the-century diesel, but a long sleek backsloped electric locomotive resting there on welded track, with the long double fin of the new 'wireless pantograph' down both sides of the loco, a genuine broadcast-power unit. Laurent and his 'uncle' boarded it, and it roared away, swiftly achieving its top speed, in the neighborhood of 200 km/h. The wheel-sound now was not *clickety-clack, clickety-clack*, but the subdued *mmmmmmmmmmmmmtchk!mmmmmmmmmmmmm* of track welded together in quarter-mile sections. The train flew, and Laurent, ecstatic, felt like he was flying with it. He waited until his 'uncle' felt more lively, then they went into the snack car. Laurent's 'uncle' got a beer and watched with a tolerant eye as Laurent went from one side to the other of the snack car, goggling out the windows. Soon enough, there came the magic moment when another train doing 200 km/h as well passed them with a *SLAM!* of displaced air and the impossible *whuffwhuffwhuffwhuffwhuff* of five cars passing in two seconds, there and gone again, as if you'd imagined them.

Oh, Pop, if you could only see this— He thought it again and again.

But *Don't waste your time worrying about me,* his father had told him after breaking the news of his departure to him, over a late-night glass of tea. *Enjoy yourself. I'll be coming after you as soon as I can. A few weeks or so . . . for I don't dare leave the project the way it is at the moment. Too many people could get hurt.* The fear had shown starkly on his father's face then, unconcealed for a moment, but a second later it was sealed away again. *Behave yourself over there, and enjoy the trip. I'll be with you soon, and there will be lots more trips like this one when we're together again . . . except when we make them, neither of us will be running.*

The fast train ran from Brasov through the towns of Deva and Arad, to Curtici at the border. As they approached this new border crossing, Laurent began to sweat again . . . then was furious at himself when they got off that train, onto another – the maglev shuttle from Lököshaza in Hungary to Wien in Austria – and the border guards at the station waved them through in complete boredom, without even bothering to look at their IDs *or* their tickets. At the station they met Laurent's 'Aunt Dina,' a small, silent dark-haired woman with a plain face and kind eyes, wearing a dull dress which looked like some kind of uniform with the insignia removed. *Who do you work for?* He wondered. *How did my pop ever set all this up, and what will they do to him if they catch him?!* But he didn't ask any of these questions out loud.

They all got on the train together, and once it was underway – Laurent's ID having once again undergone a change he didn't manage to catch happening – his name became 'Nikos,' and his 'uncle' left them, patting Laurent's shoulder and vanishing out the end of the carriage.

Laurent left his 'auntie' once, ostensibly to go to the toilet, but though he went right up to the loco end of the train and back again, he could find no sign of his 'uncle.' He couldn't imagine how the man had vanished from a moving train. Shortly, as the 'Wiener Walzer' came up to its full speed, he was once more too distracted to care very much about the whereabouts of his temporary Uncle Iolae. He was beginning to tire a little, and later what Laurent mostly recalled was how, where the track curved, he could look ahead and see birds of prey, kestrels and merlins, circling or hovering over the fields and grassland on either side of the track – waiting for the mice and other little creatures which would be frightened out of hiding by the sudden whack of air displaced by the train's passing.

They've learned the train schedule, Laurent thought. *They've found a new ecological niche for themselves, and learned how to exploit it.*

Am I going to be able to do as well without my Pop? He wondered. This new world was so strange . . . But shortly Laurent was distracted again by the MGV pulling into Wien Westbahnhof and settling down onto the track with a sigh; and 'Auntie Dina' led him over to the platform to what she told him would be the last leg of the trip – the Tunnel Train, the 'sealed' UltraGrandVitesse evacuated-maglev system which would connect under the Alps with the Swiss NEAT system, completed five years ago and the wonder of its time. This last leg would be all in the dark – but it would be only one more hour to Zurich, at near-supersonic speeds.

The train closed up and pressurized itself, levitated above the T-shaped 'podium' it rode, slipped softly out of the Westbahnhof, took itself up to 550 km/h without any fuss, and dove into the tunnel beneath the Alps. An hour later, only slowing to enter the 'vacuum-locked' part of the tunnel where it could run supersonic without having the nuisance of air pressure to deal with, the NEAT 'train' (called 'Edelweiss' after a distant wheeled ancestor) broke out of a darkness only briefly punctuated by the lights of stations where it didn't stop, and pulled up in the station below Zurich AeroSpaceport. On the far side of tube security his 'auntie' turned Laurent over to a young woman from groundside escort services, along with another ID that Laurent had never seen but had been told to expect – Hungarian, this time – and a purple EU non-resident 'transit' chip. She clasped Laurent's shoulder as she said goodbye, and he nodded and watched her go.

'Come on,' said the escort officer, and Laurent followed her. Upstairs they went from the station, ascending via three levels of escalators past a slightly unbelievable array of shops and kiosks and stores apparently selling everything on earth. Sixteen hours ago, Laurent would have goggled at it all. But now weariness and repeated spasms of fear and even a little irrational impatience were making a jaded traveler of him. What was really going to interest Laurent, now, was stopping – just standing still somewhere, sitting down somewhere that didn't move, and going no further.

He missed his father more than ever. He kept wanting to turn around and say, *Pop, Popi, look at this!* – but his father wasn't there – and then the awful thought would occur to him, *Maybe he never will be. Maybe—* But he pushed that thought aside again and again. *I'm just tired. He'll come for me as soon as he can get out . . . as soon as he can finish what he's doing.*

The airline staffer talking to him, as she led him through corridors full of bustling people, got so little by way of response that finally she gave up trying. But as they went through the last security check, which Laurent hardly noticed, she smiled just a little – and moments later they came out into the great shining curvature and acreage of the main spaceport concourse, the newest and latest-completed part of that century-old Zurich facility. Straight across the white-shining floor the view went, nearly half a mile straight through one of the biggest enclosed spaces in the world under the famous glass 'buckyball' dome, and out the far side through the world's biggest single window, to the boarding pan where not one but three 'jump' craft sat – a EuroBoeing 'hybrid' spaceplane in Swissair livery, the new Tupolev lifting body in Lufthansa gold and blue, and the 'nonhybrid' American Aerospace 'Double Eagle' spaceplane, in silver with the blue-and-red stripes.

Laurent stopped stock still and his mouth dropped open. The escort officer smiled as he looked over at her after a moment. 'That's what I thought,' she said, 'the first time I saw it.'

'Which one am I taking?' Laurent said finally.

'The AA,' said the escort officer. 'Come on. They'll preboard you, and maybe you can have a look into the cockpit before they go sterile.'

He followed her. This was everything he had imagined – a brave new world, shining, modern, new. This was what he had always wanted. All he had to do now was step out into it . . . all by himself.

Just so, proud, but (despite the airline staff) still terribly alone, Laurent Darenko – now Niko Durant – crossed the concourse into the boarding tube, into the unknown . . .

. . .and never knew how closely the eyes whose scrutiny he had most feared were watching him still.

One

It was Friday afternoon about two-thirty in Alexandria, Virginia, and in a sunny kitchen of a rambling house near the outskirts of the city, Madeline Green sat looking out of her virtual workspace, across the kitchen table, to where her mother was building a castle. Her mother swore.

'Mom,' Maj said wearily, brushing aside the piece of e-mail she had just finished answering, 'you're going to give me bad habits.' The e-mail bobbed back again, the little half-silver half-black sphere seeming to float toward her in the air – she had failed to hit the half of it that meant 'erase.' She hit the black half now, a little harder than she had intended, and the sphere popped and vanished with a small bursting-soap-bubble sound.

'Whatever habits I give you, they won't be as bad as this one,' her mother muttered. She was bent over what, from a distance, would have looked like some sort of small light-table for an artist. It had a flat square insulated plate on the bottom and a small, very bright gooseneck lamp attached to the back of the plate.

Right now her mother was holding a square of something that could have been mistaken for red-and-white-swirled plastic close under that lamp, and trying to bend it, with little success. 'Heat it up more,' Maj said.

'If I do, the colors will run,' her mother said, 'and they've run too much already. Maj honey, do me a favor and don't *ever* let Helen Maginnis talk me into another of these last-minute projects again.'

'I tried to stop you this time,' Maj said, 'but you were the one who kept saying, "Oh no, it's no problem at all, of course I'll make this big fancy centerpiece for the PTA dinner" when you said you were going to do it and now you ran out of time. Again. '

Maj's mother growled softly.

Maj laughed at her. 'This is the third time she's done this to you, Mom. And you always say you're going to let her get herself out of trouble the next time. You're just a big sucker for Helen because she's your friend.'

'Mmmf,' her mother said, and laid the piece of sugar plate back down on the heating element to re-soften. 'I don't care if it does run. The heck with perfection. You're right, honey . . .'

She turned back to her work, and Maj looked over her shoulder into her virtual space to see if any more e-mail was waiting. But the air behind her was empty, clear to the white stucco walls. Above them, through the high windows above the bookshelves and the brushed stainless-steel furniture, the remains of a furiously red-and-blue Mediterranean sunset were burning themselves out, indicating considerable heat outside on the Greek beach where the idea for this virtual workspace had originated, and more such heat tomorrow. Three years ago now, it had been, since the family had been able to synchronize both schedules and finances to go to Crete and the Greek Islands for a few weeks, and Maj sighed, wondering when they would be able to get there again. It wasn't that they were poor – not with her dad working as a tenured professor at Georgetown University, and her mom pulling down a better-than-average income as a designer of custom computer systems for big corporate clients. But having jobs as good as those also meant that both her parents seemed to be busy almost all the time, and getting everyone's vacation time into the same calendar year, let alone the same month, was a challenge. At least, with her workspace linked to the weather reports and the live Net cameras sourced in that part of the world, Maj could experience the gorgeous Greek weather vicariously, if not directly. *Maybe next year we'll go again,* she thought. *Yeah, and maybe the moon will fall down.*

She sighed. 'Workspace off,' Maj said. Immediately she felt the little hiccup in the back of her head that coincided with her implant passing the 'shutdown' order to the doubler in the kitchen, and from there to the Net-access computer in her dad's workroom. The virtual Greek villa behind Maj vanished and left her wholly in late sunlight, sitting at the big somewhat-beat-up kitchen table, watching her mother wrestling with the sugar plate. 'I don't know, Maj,' she said after a moment, 'this one might be too bumpy to be a wall. Maybe I can curl it up and make a tower out of it.'

'Maybe you should just melt it down and pour it over a waffle,' Maj said, and grinned.

'Don't tempt me . . .'

They both glanced up at the hum of a vehicle pulling up in the main parking space out in front of the house. But it was just the school bus bringing Maj's little sister home from preschool. 'I thought her dad was bringing her back today,' Maj's mother said, straightening up for a moment and massaging her back.

'No, he had something to do at the university . . .' Maj's

father's workload had increased somewhat after his tenure came through, so that Maj (and everyone else in the household) was getting used to his schedule not behaving itself, and sometimes messing theirs up as well. But at this time of year, with summer coming on fast, fortunately there was little left of Maj's schedule for her dad's to interfere with. She had finished her pre-SAT's and her finals and was waiting, not entirely calmly, for the results for the former. She had passed all the finals, and so had little left to occupy her except the music and riding that she indulged herself in while not building elaborate virtual simulations of aircraft, poking her nose into various interesting parts of the Net, and (very quietly) pursuing the studies which she intended to use to get herself into Net Force.

Which was where her heart really was, these days. Her mother sometimes looked at Maj strangely as she realized that her daughter was no longer the crazed schoolwork-fiend she had been in recent years, or rather, she was no longer studying everything that got in her way just because it did. Maj's studies now had to be more focused because Net Force mattered more than most of the other things in her life, even the hobbies she loved. That fact itself sometimes caused her mom and dad concern . . . and Maj heartily wished that they wouldn't waste the effort the concern was causing them. 'You ought to keep your options open,' her mother would say, mildly distressed. 'It's too soon to make up your mind what you're going to be doing for the rest of your life, or even the next half of it. Wait until after college,' her father would say, trying to look calm, and usually failing. All Maj would do, though, was 'Yes-Mom' or 'Yes-Dad' them because she knew what she wanted. She wanted to be in Net Force.

She was working on that already, having started, once she was allowed elective subjects in junior high, to take classes that would play to her strong suits, the things she was already good at. Mostly, Maj was good at figuring things out. Not just short-term circumstances or events, but the way a whole set of events would proceed both if left alone, and if you started tinkering with them. For a couple of years now, since she fully came to the realization that she had the beginnings of this talent, Maj had been privately 'predicting' the way events she saw on the news channels in the Net would unfold . . . and she was much heartened by the fact that the analysis-of-history and group-psych classes she had taken in her freshman and sophomore years had seemed to help the quality of her analyses. The more information you had about the world and the way it had gone before, the better you got at predicting the way it would go next. Within limits, of course, which was why Maj kept practicing the art of listening, both to others and to her own hunches. There was no way to predict what would happen if you closed yourself away from useful data by not keeping your eyes and ears open, or by looking in the wrong direction.

So Maj was concentrating on going in the right direction. She had managed to get into the Net Force Explorers – by itself, not such a shabby achievement, considering how many thousands of kids wanted in and didn't get there. Maj had some of the smartest 'Netizens' of her own age to brainstorm and network with – exploring the Net with them, looking for trouble spots, working out ways to deal with them which could be passed on to Net Force's senior staff (if you didn't manage, out of sheer cunning, to do something about a given problem yourself, and cop the credit for a good intervention). And eventually, oh, in two or three years, during or after college, she would apply to join Net Force as an adult operative . . . and they would hire her. Maj was almost sure of that. There were never enough analysts who were as interested in the world outside the Net as the world inside it, and the crucial interface where they met. That was Maj's passion – the place where real estate and 'unreal estate' met, the juncture between the physical and the virtual. People comfortable on both sides of the divide were what Net Force needed more than anything else if they were to effectively police the 'unreal' side – the fastest-growing part of the world these days, and increasingly, as thieves and terrorists and various other kinds of criminals found more and more ways to exploit it, one of the most dangerous.

That last part of the analysis, of course, was one that would have occurred to both her mother and her father before now. *But it's their job to be overprotective,* Maj thought, smiling as she heard her little sister coming up the walk outside. *In two or three years, they'll see it my way . . . especially if James Winters has asked me to join up.*

That was the only uncertainty in all this. He was a nice man, the Net Force Explorers liaison, but unpredictable, sometimes unreadable . . . even for Maj, which she found unusual. Since (having worked with her as a Net Force Explorer) he would most likely be the one to give the go/no-go decision on her hiring, she spent more time than usual wondering what was going on in his head . . . and wondering how to influence it in her favor.

The back screen door was now yanked open, and a short sturdy shape with curly blonde hair pushed in through the opening and let the door slam behind her. Maj's mother sighed. 'Adrienne, honey—' she said.

'You're just going to have to get the compressed-air

thing on the door fixed, Mom,' Maj said. 'She's only little. She can't remember not to slam it all the time.'

'She can't remember *most* of the time,' her mother said, sounding fretful as she turned back to the sugar-working lamp and plate. 'Oh, well . . .'

'C'mere, Muf,' Maj said.

Her little sister shouldered out of her knapsack, dumped it on the floor, and fixed Maj with an annoyed expression. 'I hate school,' Adrienne said. She was wearing the same stubborn expression Maj remembered her wearing the day she had decided never again to answer to the name 'Adrienne,' but only to 'Muffin.'

'No, you don't,' Maj said. 'C'mere. You mean you hate something that happened *at* school. Be precise.'

'Later,' the Muffin said, and Maj had to work not to laugh out loud. That was her father's preferred line.

'Okay,' Maj said. 'Come sit on my lap.'

This was apparently already on the Muffin's mind. She climbed up into Maj's lap and looked around her. 'Are you virtual now?'

'No, sweetie, it's turned off.'

The Muffin looked over at their mother. 'What's Mommy doing?'

'Making a castle, Muffin,' their mom said wearily. 'Or a mess.'

The Muffin looked interested until she saw the size of the stacked-up cut-out cardboard 'walls' which were templates for the plates of melted and spun sugar her mother was presently manipulating, or attempting to manipulate. 'That castle's too small for anybody to live in.'

'They could if they were pixies,' Maj said.

Maj's sister gave her a reproachful look. The Muffin believed enthusiastically in dinosaurs, but had no time for pixies, fairies, or any of various other theoretically cute life-forms infesting her storybooks or her virtual 'eduspace.'

'A bird could live there,' Muf said after a moment, apparently willing to allow Maj that much slack.

'Probably,' Maj said, resigned. She could remember when she could have gotten away with the 'pixies' remark. There were times when it seemed to her that her little sister was growing up too fast.

'It would starve,' Maj's mother said absently. She had given up on trying to make a tower out of the piece of wall she had been working with, and had managed to flatten it out properly. Now she finished affixing that piece of wall to the plate-sugar base waiting for it, and having done so she leaned against the counter while she waited for the next piece of sugar plate to heat. 'Birds can't eat sugar, Muf.'

'No. It would rot their teeth,' said the Muffin with the world-weary air of someone who had heard this concept entirely too often.

'Birds don't have teeth,' Maj said.

'They did when they were dinosaurs,' said the Muffin, and smiled, looking slightly feral.

There was no arguing with such a statement, and it was probably wiser not to try to anyway.

'Where's Daddy?' the Muffin now demanded. 'He said he would take me to the park when he came home.'

'If he's much later, I'll take you, Muf,' Maj said. 'I think he's late at school.'

'Why? Was he bad?'

'No,' Maj said. 'Usually they keep Daddy late at school because he's good.'

'Hah,' her mother remarked in deep irony. She had her own opinions about Maj's dad's tendency to overwork, and to allow himself to be overworked when what he thought of as the good of his students was at stake.

The Muffin was still reacting to what seemed the illogic of Maj's statement. 'Bobby Naho,' she said, 'threw his clay at Mariel and they made *him* stay after and be counseled.'

'I promise you that Daddy hasn't thrown his clay at anybody,' Maj said. 'Though I bet he'd like to sometimes.'

'I'm going to wash up for going to the park,' said the Muffin abruptly, and vanished into the rambling depths of the house.

Maj's mother turned to watch this with some interest. '*That's* a new development,' she said.

'Yeah, Muf has it all figured out. Wash for going-out, and going-out has to happen.'

'She's discovered causality,' her mother said, and sighed. 'We're all doomed.'

Another high whine from outside made them both turn their heads again. This time it was one that Maj immediately recognized – her dad's car.

Maj stretched and got up to put the kettle on the stove for a cup of tea. Shortly afterwards she heard the front door open, and the sound of keys and briefcases being dropped here and there, away up in the front hall. Maj's house was a long one, built in stages over some decades, and it straggled somewhat, so that the distance between the front hall and the kitchen was not *really* long enough to require you to take a packed lunch with you, but seemed so (especially when the kitchen phone went off and you had to run for it). After a little while Maj's dad came through the kitchen door and paused there, looking at what his wife was doing at the counter.

'You'll never have that done in time,' he said, while the Muffin screeched 'Daddy! Daddy!' down the hallway, and abruptly impacted into his legs from behind, making him wobble.

'Wanna bet?' Maj's mother said, not looking up. 'We're due there at eight thirty. The question is, will you have done the laundry so you have a clean shirt?'

'Was it my turn? Sorry, I forgot. Things got hectic.' He picked up the Muffin in one arm. 'Yes, I know. The park,' Maj's father said to her, and leaned against the doorpost. From there he looked at Maj, the overhead light shining off his bald spot. 'Well, guess what.'

There was something odd about the way he looked as he said this, though his face was cheerful enough, and Maj watched him carefully as she said, 'What?'

'We've got company coming.'

'How are they at house-tidying?' said Maj's mother, wrestling with the next piece of sugar plate. 'Because I'm not going to have time.'

'No, it's not right now. And I don't think we need to do anything special. It's family.'

Her mother turned with a surprised look. 'Oh? Who?'

'Not close family,' Maj's father said, putting the Muffin down again. 'Go get your park toy, honey,' he said, 'just one.'

'Okay. Who's coming?' Muffin said. 'Are you getting me a little brother finally?'

Maj grinned and turned to get the kettle off the stove. This had been a recurrent theme of late, since Muffin's preschool classes had started a 'family life' unit. 'Muffy, don't give them ideas,' Maj said. 'You don't know how lucky we are to have just *one* brother. We've got him outnumbered . . . let's keep it that way. But Dad, who is it?'

'A third cousin . . . I think.'

'Mom's side of the family?' It was the usual assumption.

28

Her mother was the youngest of seven kids now scattered all over the planet, and one attempt some years back to count all the resulting cousins and second cousins had been the only reason Maj got to stay up late enough at one of her aunt's weddings to see her uncle Mike dance something he called the 'Funky Chicken' on the head table. They had finally stopped counting at something like eighty cousins, and after hitting a hundred in the second-cousin count, everyone had given up and gone back to watching Uncle Mike.

'That's right,' her father said. He looked over at her mother and said, 'Elenya called me today – she couldn't reach you, apparently.'

Elenya was one of Maj's mom's cousins, a cartographer who now lived in Austria with her formerly Hungarian husband and worked for the Austrian national cartographic service. 'Oh, gosh,' Maj's mother said, 'I've been in and out all day . . . She didn't leave a message in the system, though.'

'No, I guess when she couldn't reach you, she figured she would catch me at work. Anyway, the visitor in question is one of *her* second cousins, a youngster named Niko. Apparently his father is getting ready for a relocation from Hungary to the States, and their apartment is having to be closed up before the new one here is ready. School's done there already, and there's nowhere for the youngster to go. Elenya wanted to know if we had room and inclination to put him up for a few weeks until his father arrives to take charge of him.'

'Of course we do,' Maj's mother said. 'That's what spare rooms are for.' She glanced up. 'Is he English-speaking?'

'Fairly fluent, apparently.'

Maj was trying to make an image in her mind of exactly

29

how the newcomer's relationship to her own family would look if set up as a 'family tree' diagram, and failing. 'So if he's Mom's cousin's second cousin . . . that makes him a . . . third cousin . . . twice removed?'

'Something like that,' Maj's father said, looking bemused. 'The "removal" thing always confuses me. Anyway, his father will come and pick him up after he's finished tying up some loose ends of his business back in Hungary.'

'Wow, Hungary, that's exotic,' Maj said. She grinned. 'This Niko kid . . . is he cute?'

Her father cleared his throat and gave her one of Those Looks. 'A little young for you, Maj. He's thirteen.'

'Will he play with me?' the Muffin demanded at the top of her lungs.

'How could anybody not play with you, you curly thing?' Maj's father said, holding the Muffin out at arms' length and shaking her around. The Muffin squealed with delight. He put her down and said, 'Now, go on, get the park toy! We won't have a lot of time, I have to get back . . .'

'. . . and do the laundry,' Maj's mother said as the Muffin ran off for her toy.

'Rub it in, you slave driver,' Maj's father said, a little wearily, and ran one hand over where his hair wasn't any more.

The Muffin's yells of excitement receded down the hall. 'Is this going to be okay for you, Maj?' her father said. 'He'll need some attention – I don't want him to feel left out.'

'Dad,' Maj said, 'don't worry about it. Thirteen's kind of young, but just because he's younger doesn't by itself make him a nuisance. And besides, there's the Net. He'll either bring stuff with him that he's interested in, or he'll get at his home server through ours.'

Her father nodded. Again Maj caught that faintly worried look. Once might have been accidental, or caused by something else, but twice?

There's something about this he's not telling me, Maj thought. *Telling* us—

'When's he getting in, hon?' Maj's mother said, not turning around, still wrestling with the sugar plate.

'Tomorrow, around noon,' her father said. 'It's an AA flight into Baltimore-Washington. No point in making him take the train down. He'll be wrecked as it is – he'll have had a long trip. I thought I'd go up and get him.'

'You're an angel,' Maj's mother said, and turned around to kiss him soundly, holding her sticky-gloved hands up and away like a surgeon avoiding becoming nonsterile.

'I'll go with you,' Maj said.

Her father smiled slightly, but there was just a little something missing about the smile. 'Going to lay down the law early, huh?'

'I might not need to,' Maj said, and smiled. 'But if he starts acting up, well, better get the corrective measures started right away.'

Her father chuckled and turned to head back down the hall to the bedroom end of the house. 'Let me change out of this shirt,' he said. 'If there's anything else that needs to be washed, make a pile in the hall. Muffin, you ready . . .?'

Maj went to get herself a mug for her tea, and went fishing in the canister on the window for a teabag, while for the moment keeping her face turned away from her mother's. *What's going on . . .?* she wondered. It wasn't that sudden guests from strange places were unusual. In this house, they weren't.

What *wasn't* usual was her father looking afraid . . .

31

★　★　★

'There is nothing we can do at the moment,' said the tense voice down the other end of the comm line. 'We caught the identity shifts they pulled, finally . . . but too late. He's gone.'

In the plain, bare little office, with its two pieces of steel furniture and the peeling beige paint on the walls, Major Elye Arni swore softly under her breath. Outside the office, things got very quiet. Her assistants knew better than to bother her at such times. 'How did it happen?'

'Apparently someone got him fake ID that was good enough to get through our border systems. Then the boy was picked up and taken out of immediate surveillance range by an escort previously unknown to us.'

'He'll be known *now*, though,' she said, her voice grim with threat.

'Oh, yes, Major, we'll have him shortly,' said the voice on the other end of comms.

He would have to say that, the Major thought . . . both out of fear of what she would be thinking, and from fear of who was probably listening somewhere else on the line. It was always assumed, and wisely, that someone Higher Up was listening to whatever you were discussing, and even at times when she knew this not to be true, the Major did not dissuade any of her associates from believing it. It was healthy for them to be scared. It kept them honest. Or as honest as they were capable of being.

'We'll see,' Major Arni said. 'I tell you, I don't know where all these subversives keep coming from. You'd think we'd have shaken them all out after twenty years, but no . . . Ingrates. So where exactly is the boy now?'

'Over the mid-Atlantic. He'll be landing in a couple of hours.'

'And you'll have someone to meet him at the other end, I take it.'

'Oh, of course, Major. It's just that—' He sounded suddenly unnerved.

'Just that *what?*'

'Well,' said her subordinate, 'we can't just grab him at the airport, I'm afraid. Their security is too tight.'

She started to get annoyed. 'Surely the airport security people don't know anything about him that would alert them to any need for extra vigilance! He's just a boy. And not even the son of anyone particularly important.'

'No, it's not that, Major, of course they don't know about him.' Her subordinate was flustered. 'But the Western countries are all so paranoid about their children being kidnapped, or snatched by parents feuding over a divorce settlement, or by some prowling sex maniac, that a child in transit can't be turned over to anyone but the person they've been "sent" to. The airlines are strict about it. There have been lawsuits, and they—'

'If you think I have time to waste hearing about the mendacities of some corrupt Western legal system,' the Major said, 'you're much mistaken. Send someone who can pass for the person picking the boy up.'

'Major, we can't; the authorities there will be checking the collecting adult's ID by retinal scan.'

She swore again. There were ways to fake that, these days, but not in time, and this little fish didn't justify that kind of expense . . . yet. 'Who exactly *is* picking the boy up?'

'We think it must be someone involved with one of the national intelligence organizations, Major. Why Washington, otherwise?'

She wasn't convinced. 'They could pick him up anywhere,' the Major muttered. 'It wouldn't necessarily have to be there.' She brooded for a moment. 'Does the father possibly know anybody in that area?'

'It's a possibility. He studied there for a while,' said her subordinate.

The Major frowned. 'In *America*? What was a loyal scientist from our country doing there?'

'Please, Major, it's all too common. He was sent there by the government years ago, some student-exchange program, to "learn about their culture"—'

'To poach their science, you mean,' she growled, 'and to give their damned intelligence services a chance to try and suborn him.' Still, she knew this kind of thing had gone on a lot in the last thirty years – people being sent overseas to get at the improved equipment and theory which the Western countries had refused to allow her country to import honestly, citing 'human rights record problems' and other fabricated excuses to keep their enemies poor and technologically inferior. Well, in this particular case, it hadn't worked. The CIA and its cluster of other associated intelligence agencies had hit Darenko and bounced. He simply wasn't interested in being a double agent, it seemed . . . too interested in just doing science. And now Darenko's work was proving unusually useful for the government. Everything about it had seemed to be going extremely well, there had been great hopes for the results of his newest research . . . until now.

The Major felt like growling a lot louder. You gave people better than usual housing and salaries, rewarded them with high position and the favor of the government and the national defense establishments, and what did they do? Turn on you at the first opportunity. *What does he mean sending his son off to the West like this?* Except she knew perfectly well what was meant by it. He was getting ready to jump, and – smart man that he was – he knew that sending his son off alone increased their chances of a reunion later. Together, their escape would have been almost impossible. Yet by sending the boy away, he had also telegraphed his own intentions. He would shortly find out how big an error that had been.

She let out a long breath. 'Well,' Major Arni said, 'what do you know about the person picking him up?'

'Uh . . . nothing as yet.'

The Major's eyes narrowed. 'You must be able to find out *something!* There must be information about the person's identity attached to the boy's ticketing information in the airline's computers.'

'We tried that,' her subordinate said. 'Unfortunately we couldn't hack into the ticketing system. The air ticket "audit trail" starts in Zurich, and the Swiss computers' encryption—'

'*I don't want to hear about their encryption!*' she yelled. 'Damned paranoid Swiss, *why* are they so secretive?' She let out a long breath of annoyance. 'Stupid little mob of hold-up-your-hand-and-vote democrats—'

The Major bit off the diatribe, which would have served no purpose, and would just have re-inflamed slightly raw nerves anyway. Some months ago, someone from her department had been caught bugging the new French Embassy building in Bern, and had been ejected by the Swiss within six hours. No appeal, no chance to get someone in there to finish the job, just a lot of embarrassment which she was still living down. She was fortunate not to have been reassigned, and the incident still rankled. Meanwhile, the terrified silence at the other end of the phone was amusing.

'All right,' she said at last. 'Fine. I don't suppose you

have anyone on the plane, someone who could get cozy with one of the flight attendants and get a look at the boy's travel documents?'

'Uh, no, Major. On such short notice we couldn't get the disbursements office to authorize the funds for a 'jump' flight. That kind of expense, they want an application filed in sextuplicate a month beforehand.' He sounded bitter, and didn't bother concealing it. And this time the Major was inclined to agree with him, although she really had no business complaining about it to her. One of the perpetual annoyances of her job was the tiny budget on which she was required to produce decent results. *How am I supposed to defend the security of my country on a shoestring?* But hard currency was just that, hard to come by, and there was no one she could complain to either, not without hurting her own position, for such complaints were likely to be taken as evidence of insufficient motivation, or (much worse) incipient treachery.

She sighed. 'So what you're telling me,' the Major said, 'is that all we can do is watch to see who picks the boy up at the Washington end. And if it's the CIA, or Net Force, or some other government organization, then that's the end of everything, is it?'

'Oh, no, Major. Even they get clumsy sometimes. One slip in their security is all we need.' She could hear him almost smiling a little on the other end of the link, and maybe he was right to do so. 'And besides, his father has to try to follow shortly. The "collectors" on that side themselves are likely to tip us off, just by whatever preparations they make. When the father does try to follow, we'll catch him and squeeze him dry. *He'll* certainly know where the boy was headed. Either way, we'll have them both back in short order . . . or make them useless to the other side.'

'You'd better hope it works out that way,' the Major said. 'I want a report as soon as that plane comes down. Who picked him up, who they work for, where they take him. I want him taken back at the earliest opportunity. And, Taki – make a note – if anyone slips and kills him, they'll be just as dead within hours. This isn't just some schoolboy. We need him intact.'

'Ah,' said the voice on the other end. 'Pressure . . .'

'Oh, certainly. What father likes to see his son's finger-nails pulled off with pliers in front of him?' said the Major idly. 'Though I doubt we'd have to do more than one or two. And if the boy turns out to be innocent, of course we'd compensate him afterwards. The Government has to defend itself from spies and terrorists, but it doesn't prey on innocent citizens.'

'Of course,' said the voice on the other end, rather hurriedly. 'Will there be anything else, Major?'

'Just that report in two hours, or when the plane comes down, whichever comes sooner. See to it.'

He hurriedly clicked off. She put down the comm handpiece at her end.

Innocent citizens, the Major thought. *Are there any?*

Personally, she doubted it. It was just as well. It made her job easier.

She looked out the office door. None of her staff were stirring. 'Come on,' she said, raising her voice, 'look lively out there! Rosa, I want the schedules for the American Aerospace planes into Reagan and Dulles and BWI for the next six hours. With the "possible diversion" variants. Check the weather to see if a diversion is likely at all. And get me the last list of our Washington assets—'

Out in the office, she could hear them starting to bustle around again. She sat there for a few moments more in silence – a little slender blonde-haired woman in uniform, her hair pulled back in the regulation twist, her hands folded, looking thoughtful. *Ingrates*, she was thinking again. *A pity they need you alive.*

Though, once they make sure we've got all your work complete, it's not as if you're likely to be that way for long . . .

Two

For Maj, the previous evening had pretty much been routine. Maj's Mom and Dad left at eight thirty for the PTA dinner, with Maj's mother bearing before her an astonishingly detailed medieval castle rendered in sugar plate, right down (or up) to small spun-sugar banners flying from toothpicks fixed in the battlements. The Muffin went off to play in virtual space until bedtime, and Maj sat at the kitchen table for a good while, snacking on a pomegranate while going through her piled-up e-mail and occasionally looking out of her own workspace through a 'side door' she had installed into Muffin's virtual 'play area,' a large green woodland meadow which at the moment was populated by a number of deinonichuses, iguanas, and very small stegosaurs. In the middle of this pastoral landscape the Muffin was sitting on a large smooth rock and reading to the assorted saurians, very slowly, carefully sounding out the words. '. . . And the great serpent said, "What has brought thee to this island, little one? Speak quickly, and if thou dost not ac-quaint me with something I have not heard, or knew not before, thou shalt van—, vanish like a flame—" '

Maj smiled and turned her attention back to the electronic mail that 'lay' all over the kitchen table, or bobbled around in the air in front of her in the form of various brightly-colored three-dimensional icons. A lot of it was in the form of shiny black spheres of baseball size, with the number 7 flashing inside it – mail from her friends in that wildly assorted loose association, the 'Group of Seven.' There were actually a lot more than seven of them, now, but as a group they were too lazy to bother changing the number every time someone new joined. They had other things to think about – one of them, at the moment, being a new 'sim' that presently had a lot of other people on the Net interested as well.

Maj and the other members of the Group had originally started getting together on a regular basis because they were all interested in designing their own sims-simulated realities, 'playrooms' or 'pocket universes' based in the Net, where you could lose an hour or a week engaged in conversation, or combat, with other people – a few of them, or thousands. For a lucky few with the necessary talent and perseverance, it could become a career, an incredibly lucrative one, and some of the Group of Seven had this kind of future in mind for themselves. They designed sims, and let the rest of the Group play with them, 'test-driving' them and working out the kinks. It was 'practicing for the real world' for these kids. Others, like Maj, just liked to play 'inside' small custom-designed sims rather than the big glossy ones, which tended to be expensive.

But every now and then one came along that was caused an unusual amount of interest. *Cluster Rangers* was one of these. It was a space sim – the latest of what, over the course of the life of the Net, had probably been thousands of space-oriented games, puzzles, and virtual environments. But there was something rather special about this one. It wasn't just that Mihail Oranief, the sim designer, had taken incredible care over the details, which by itself was hardly unusual. It was a big, juicy, complex game, full of interesting solar systems, weird alien races, and interesting characters having interesting (and occasionally fatal) conflicts with one another.

Cluster Rangers had a couple of additional attractions that had seemed to drop out of a lot of space sims, or were never in them at all. For one thing, it was very interactive. Not just in the obvious sense, that you got into it and lived it for hours at a time. But Oranief had seen fit to release his 'interface code,' the 'modular' programming which would allow players to design their own spacecraft, space stations, even their own planets, and 'plug them into' the *Cluster Rangers* universe.

This by itself was both a courtesy and a challenge – the sign of a very assured and confident programmer who was willing to let people enter his universe and make it even better. And that by itself had powerfully attracted Maj and most of the rest of the Seven – all eleven of them. For some weeks now they had jointly been engaged in the design of a small squadron of fighter craft which would make their debut at the upcoming Battle of Didion, presently scheduled for tomorrow night.

All of them were determined to make a splash, and they had come up with what they considered the ultimate small fighter craft for exploiting the laws of science as the sim designer had laid them down. There were some big differences there from the average virtual universe. Light-speed was much lower, and the human body could stand more G's, but to Maj's mind, the most amusing change was that, though there was vacuum, it also conducted sound and when you blew something up, you heard the *BOOM!* without breaking any rules. There were people

41

who despised this warping of conventional physical reality as excessive whimsy. For her own part, Maj was willing to cut the sim designers a small amount of slack. She liked the booms.

But ship design was what was primarily occupying her and the rest of the Group at the moment. All these mails now piled up on Maj's 'desk' involved last-minute changes to the craft – suggestions and alterations, ideas picked up and immediately discarded, rude remarks about other people's ideas (or one's own), bad jokes, fits of nervousness or excitement, and various expressions of scorn, panic, or self-satisfaction. The Group had picked a side to align itself with in the Battle, had made some new friends and some new enemies, and was, Maj judged, pretty much ready to get out there now and go head-to-head with some of the Archon's 'Black Arrow' squadrons. Their own 'Arbalest' ships were both effective and handsome – a point about which, considering the quality of the rest of the game, Maj had had some concern.

Most designers who simply adapted astronomical photos from the Hubble and Alpher-Bethe-Gamow Space telescopes for their scenarios wound up, despite the sometimes spectacular nature of the images, with backgrounds that looked hard and cold. Maj wasn't sure what Oranief had done to his 'exteriors,' but they somehow looked hard and *warm*. It was an unusual distinction, this ability to make space, already beautiful enough, look even more so, to make blackness more than just black, but also dark and mysterious, and either threateningly so – so that you looked over your shoulder nervously while you were flying – or *kindly* so, so that you hung there in the darkness with a feeling that something approved of you being there. However Oranief did it, the effect of *Cluster Rangers*, the sense of *depth* in a game, of it all meaning more somehow than it looked like it did, was like nothing else on the Net, and people had been flocking to join the sim as a result. Maj was glad that she and the Group had gotten in early, since there was talk of the designer closing down admissions soon and limiting the number of users to those who had already signed up.

She sighed and put the last mail aside, a panicky voicemail from Bob, who had been complaining that he wasn't sure the camber of the wings on the Arbalest craft was deep enough. Maj recognized this for what it was – last-minute nerves. 'Mail routine,' she said.

'Running, boss,' said her workspace in a pleasant, neutral female voice.

'Start reply. Bobby, baby,' Maj said, 'if you think I for one am going to support you in yet another change of design the day before the balloon goes up, you're out of your mind. We have a beautiful ship. We are going to beat the butts off the Black Arrows when they come after us.' *When* – the thought made the hair on the back of Maj's neck prickle a little, for there was something inhumanly *nasty* about the way the Black Arrows flew – too quick to be affected by G's, too merciless in the aftermath of an attack. There were rumors in the game that the Black Arrow craft were flown by the undead . . . and it was also rumored that Free Fighter squadrons should do anything to avoid being taken alive by their enemies, lest they get that way themselves. *Not that we've seen that many squads survive an attack by them in the first place,* she thought . . . 'So just weld your spinal vertebrae together for the time being and play the man. We're going to be fine. Signed, Maj. End mail.'

'Queue or immediate send?' said Maj's workspace.

'Send.' She sighed, glanced up. 'Time?'

'Nine sixteen p.m.'

'Oh, gosh, and the Muf is still up,' Maj said to herself. She got up, plucked the icon-sphere of the last e-mail from Bob out of the air, picked up the remaining ones from where they lay on the table, and strolled over to the 'filing cabinet' where she kept the *Cluster Rangers* material – a virtual 'box' the shape of an Arbalest fighter. She pulled up the canopy of the fighter and stuffed the little message-spheres down into it, then closed the canopy and took one last look at the fighter's design. The beautifully backslanted wings were perfect, even though they were more often than not superfluous. The fighter spent most of its time in deep space. Still, the group had built into the ship the ability to go atmospheric if necessary – it was intended to be an ace-in-the-hole. Not many designers retained that capability, opting instead to use shuttlecraft or transporter platforms for their on-planet work. In the upcoming battle, conditions were ripe to exploit the ship's versatility.

' "Camber",' she muttered. 'Bob needs his head examined.'

She turned toward the 'door' into the Muffin's space, and headed through it. Muffin was still sitting on her rock and reading to the dinosaurs – one particularly large stegosaur was looking over her shoulder, while chewing a mouthful of grass.

Do they really eat *grass?* Maj wondered.

'And the woodcutter said—'

Maj peered over the Muffin's shoulder briefly. 'Come on, you,' she said. 'Bedtime.'

There was a general groan of annoyance from the dinosaurs. Way up above her, a tyrannosaur bent down and showed its teeth. 'Yeah, you, too,' Maj said, unimpressed, waving a hand in front of her face. 'Wow, when did you brush last?'

'It's not my fault,' the tyrannosaur said. 'I eat people.'

'Yeah, well, you could try flossing in between meals,' said Maj, wondering once more who was doing the programming for these creatures. They were *somebody's* sim, and theoretically came from someone who had been qualified to write sims for small children, though at moments like this Maj wondered exactly what those qualifications looked like. At any rate, she doubted they were doing the Muffin any particular harm. Her little sister was in some ways unusually robust.

'I didn't finish the story,' the Muffin said, annoyed.

'Okay,' Maj said. 'Finish it up. Then bedtime.'

The Muffin opened her book. The dinosaurs leaned down again. 'And the woodcutter chopped the wolf open, and Little Red Riding Hood and her grandmother fell out. Then the woodcutter took great stones and put them in the wolf's belly, and sewed the wolf up again, and threw it in the lake, and it never came back up. And the kindly woodcutter took Red Riding Hood home to her mother and father, who cried and laughed when they saw her, and made her promise never to go into the woods by herself again.'

The Muffin closed the book, and the dinosaurs stood up around her with a kind of sigh of completion. 'Good night,' Muffin said to them, and there was a chorus of grunts and hoots and growls, and they all stalked off among the trees, where darkness began to fall.

Maj suddenly began to wonder why she had been bothering to worry about the saurians. *Chopping wolves open, stuffing them with stones, and throwing them in lakes—?! I don't remember that being in the story I read.* But then it had been a long time ago . . . 'All done?' she said to the Muffin, picking her up.

'All done,' said Muffin. The virtual landscape faded away, replaced by Maj's little sister's bedroom.

Maj got the Muffin into her pajamas and put her in bed. 'What did you make of that story, small stuff?' Maj said.

'I didn't make it. It was there.'

'I mean, what do you *think* it meant?'

'That you shouldn't go into the forest by yourself, or talk to strangers,' the Muffin said. 'Unless you're a grownup, or you have an axe. And it's very bad to kill people, or eat people. Unless you're a dinosaur and can't help it.'

Maj blinked. 'And that last bit, about the stones?'

'The wolf had it coming,' said the Muffin.

Maj choked on a laugh. 'Oh,' she said. 'You want a drink of water?'

'No.'

'Okay, honey. You have a good sleep.'

'Night night,' said the Muffin, and turned over and snuggled down among the covers.

Maj softly shut the door to her room and decided that she didn't have to bother worrying about her sister's relationship with the virtual dinosaurs. The Brothers Grimm, though, might be another matter, though in this area as well the Muffin seemed to be handling things her own way, calmly and with a certain panache.

She chuckled and made the rounds of the house, checking the locks before turning in. She had an early morning coming up, and then there would be this new kid, Niko, to deal with as well. *As long as his being here doesn't interfere with the sim,* she thought, *everything should be fine . . .*

★   ★   ★

Six in the morning came all too early. It was not Maj's idea of a normal time to get up, but some of the Group of Seven were on the pacific coast, and this was the time of day and/or night when it was easiest to get everyone together.

All the same, she was not going to go virtual at such an hour without at least a little preparation. She strolled out to the kitchen in her bathrobe, rubbing her eyes, and put the kettle on, then went back down the hall, hearing a voice – her mother's, she thought.

By her mother's office door she stopped and listened. No sound – the voice she had heard was coming down the hall from the master bedroom.

Some early morning Net show, she thought. Her father was addicted to them at any hour of the day or night.

However, a little light seeped under her mother's office door. Maj knocked softly – no answer. She opened the door very quietly, peeked in.

Her mother was leaning back in her implant chair, her eyes closed. The chair began to hum as she stood there, going into a 'massage' cycle to keep her mother's muscles from getting cramped up while she worked.

Maj backed out and shut the door. As late as they had been out last night, there was no keeping her mother away from her work, even at a weekend. 'When I sell a system, honey,' her mother kept saying, 'I sell service, too. That's why they keep coming back to me.' And indeed Maj knew her mother's systems were well thought of in the DC area. She had at least one small government contract, which she didn't discuss, and many other contracts for various firms in the District and the tri-state area. *I just wish these people wouldn't screw their systems up after Mom installs them,* Maj

47

thought, *so that she has to keep fixing them* . . .

She headed on down to the bathroom. Her brother's bedroom door, which she passed on the way, was open just a crack. She could hear a faint snore coming from inside. *Another late night for him,* Maj thought. But this time of year, that was normal. He and his curling buddies often didn't finish a 'weekend' training session until midnight, after which they would go to one of the all-night diners down in Alexandria and eat and drink until two or sometimes three. Her brother claimed that it was amazing the way curling took the energy out of you. It was all mindwork, he claimed – nothing to do with the mere physical exertion involved, which mostly involved scooting up and down a lane of ice, brushing it with brooms and shouting occasionally off-color suggestions to a large polished rock. Maj had her doubts about the 'mindwork' aspects of this sport, or how much energy it took out of you. But she didn't bother voicing them to her brother, who sometimes claimed that there couldn't possibly be any energy expended while playing a viola. *Like he has the slightest idea* . . .

She brushed her teeth while waiting for the kettle to go off, and as she finished and came out of the bathroom, she caught that murmur of sound again, from the main bedroom . . . Not a show. Her father's voice. He was using the 'repeater' in the bedroom to hook into the main Net computer in his study, and talking to somebody. *At this hour?* But then again, in Europe it was lunchtime. If it was something to do with their new guest . . .

Maj started to turn away, then paused. She was not a big eavesdropper, normally, but there was something about the timbre of her father's voice that made her stop and stand still right where she was, straining to hear better without going any closer.

'. . . Yes. Yes, I know, but I didn't feel that I had much choice. He's a friend, Jim. If you don't help your friends when they need it, then there's not much point in the concept of friendship to begin with.'

Maj had been about to step away from the door, rather embarrassed at her own eavesdropping, until she heard the name 'Jim.' There were only two people whom her father addressed that way. One was an uncle in Denver, his brother. The other was James Winters, the Net Force Explorers liaison. Considering what time it was in Denver, Maj thought she could guess which one it was.

'Yes, I know. Well, it's a done deal. He's about to arrive. I would have liked to give you more warning but, when it all started, any more communication between him and me might have tipped off the very people he was trying to avoid. And then I couldn't get you last night.'

A long silence. 'Of course we will,' her father said. 'Maj is good that way.' And another pause. 'Yes, around ten. We should have gotten him home by then, assuming the traffic's not too bad. Right. Till then.'

She blushed and moved off quietly down the hall. Bad enough to hear yourself being complimented while you were being a sneak and listening to people's private conversations, or half of them.

But this kid coming in, this Nick, is one of our relatives. Why would Dad be talking to James Winters about him . . .?

She went back up the hall toward the kitchen, listening for the kettle. It was grumbling to itself, not ready to whistle yet. At the door of her dad's study Maj paused, was briefly overcome by one more yawn, then wandered in to look at some of the books and paperwork piled up on the work table in vast quantities, as usual. Some of them were quite old – 'Eastern European studies' stuff, bound magazines in various East European languages, some in Cyrillic lettering and some in Roman, some of them fifty, maybe sixty years old. Somehow Maj started to get the idea that all this stuff was not anything to do with coursework.

She wandered back out again and into the kitchen, where the kettle's grumbling and rumbling was getting louder, and thought about her relatives. The Greens had relations all over the western part of Europe – Ireland, mostly, and some in France and Spain and Austria. She had been surprised to find that some of them had married into the famous Lynch winemaking family, Irish emigrants who had settled in Bordeaux in the 1800s and had been deep in viticulture ever since. *Eastern Europe, though,* Maj thought. *No one ever mentioned before that we had anybody out that way. Weird . . .*

Unless we don't *really have anyone out that way.*

The kettle began to whimper, preparatory to breaking into full cry, and Maj reached up to open one of the cupboards and get a teabag of the Japanese green tea with roasted rice that she favored, then she got a mug off the mug tree. That her father was on the link to James Winters was in itself odd enough. Not that she didn't know that they were friends. Apparently they had been at school together at some point. But why would her dad be discussing their visitor with *him . . .?*

Unless this new kid is Net Force business somehow—

Which made it, as far as Maj was concerned, her business as well . . . especially when it turned up in her own household.

The kettle started to shriek. Maj pulled it hurriedly off the burner and poured the boiling water onto her teabag, then killed the burner and took the mug over to the table, sat down with it. A moment later her mother came scuffing in, also wearing that slightly beat-up 'work bathrobe' she favored for these early morning work sessions, a garish multicolored thing she had brought back from Covent Garden in London after a consulting trip. 'These people,' she muttered, making for the same cupboard Maj had opened, and taking out a one-shot coffee dripper. 'I build them a system that works like a dream, but can they leave it alone? Noooo. They have to tinker with it, and attach new programs to it, and they don't debug the programs, and then they wonder why the whole thing crashes . . .'

'Morning, Mom,' Maj said.

'Morning, honey,' her mother said. 'Thank you for not saying "good".'

Maj was itching to ask her mother why her dad would be on the phone to James Winters . . . but that would reveal that she had been eavesdropping.

'Daddy up yet?' her mother said.

'I think so. Sounded like he was on the link or something.'

'The man just won't rest.'

'Neither will *you*.'

'And what are *you* doing up this hour?' her mother said. 'Before you accuse *us* of being incorrigible workaholics.'

'Oh, our big space battle's tonight. Prebriefing.'

'That serious?' her mother said, pouring water into the prepacked coffee filter.

'Well, we've spent a lot of time on development,' Maj said. 'We don't want to get immediately dead because we didn't discuss what we were going to *do* with what we developed.'

'Mmm,' her mother said then. 'No argument there . . .'

They sat in companionable silence for a while and drank

their tea and coffee respectively. After a few moments, there came a faint *tick!* From one side of the kitchen. Maj's mom cocked her head. 'Aha,' she said, for the *tick!* had come from the water heater. 'He's in the shower, then.'

Maj's father would have lived in the shower if he was allowed to. He claimed he got his best ideas there. Maj's thought was that it was probably best that he had a day job which kept him out of the shower occasionally. Otherwise he would now quite likely rule the world. 'I'm in no rush,' she said. 'I was going to go to this meeting first.'

'Good.' Her mother had another slurp of coffee. 'Honey, about our little guest . . .'

'Mmmh?'

'You do realize that he's—'

'*Mommy, mommy, look what I found!*'

The Muffin, horribly awake for this hour of the day, came charging into the kitchen, waving a tattered picture book. Maj sighed. Whatever the manufacturers said about these books being 'child-proof,' they had not yet run them past the Muffin.

'—Thirteen,' her mother said after a moment, looking slightly bemused.

'Oh, yeah, Mom, it's no problem,' Maj said. 'I'll manage.'

'It was lost,' the Muffin said, 'and I found it under my bed.' She waved the book under her mother's nose. It had an earnest-looking dinosaur on the cover.

'That's where most things go,' said Maj, who had previous experience in this regard with her little sister. The Muffin regarded 'under the bed' as a storage area of infinite flexibility.

'Will you read it to me, Mommy?'

'But you can read it yourself, sweetie,' her mother said, wearily taking another swig of coffee.

'It's good to read to people,' the Muffin insisted. '*I* read to my dinosaurs. It makes them smarter.'

Maj and her mother gave each other an amused look. 'Well, honey,' her mother started to say, and then the phone rang.

'Now, who can it be at this hour?' her mother said, looking up. 'They'd better not be expecting imagery, because they're not going to get it. Hello?' she said.

The Muffin looked annoyed, and wandered over to the other side of the table with the book, where she climbed up on a chair, slapped the book down on the table and began to read aloud to herself.

'No,' Maj's mother said to the air over the recitation of dinosaur names, 'he's not available at the moment; may I take a message for him? —Yes, this is Mrs Green. —Oh. —Oh. And it's landing where?'

There was a pause. 'Seven fifteen? There wasn't any problem with the plane, was there?'

Maj's eyebrows went up. '–Oh, well that's good,' her mother said. 'No problem. Yes, we'll be there. Thank you! Bye now!'

She blinked, 'hanging up,' and turned to Maj. 'So much for the virtues of getting up early and having half an hour to relax,' she muttered, and glanced at the Muffin. 'They've diverted our young cousin's flight to Dulles.'

'Isn't that good for us, though? We don't have to go all the way down to BWI.'

'It would be good if he wasn't landing in three-quarters of an hour,' her mother said, getting up and swigging down the rest of her coffee at a rate that made Maj wonder one more time if her mother had a heat shield for a throat. 'Better get dressed, honey, we've got a plane to meet.'

'Ohmigosh,' Maj said. 'My meeting with the Group—!'

'You're going to have to abort it,' her mother said. 'This is family stuff, hon, sorry . . . I think you're needed. Tell them you'll talk to them later.'

'It wasn't just a talk, it was—!'

But her mother was already on her way down the hall, and a second later she was banging on the bathroom door, shouting, 'Sweetie, the sky is falling, better come out of there!'

Maj heard a strangled noise come through the faint sound of rushing water. Reluctantly she got up and went off to get dressed, after which she would have to rush to commandeer enough time on the computer to tell the group she was going to have to miss out on the briefing. *They're going to be furious. Come to think of it, I think I'm furious.*

So much for this little Niko not interfering with anything, Maj thought as she stalked off down the hallway. *What a wonderful time we're going to have together . . .*

Fortunately, it being the awful hour of the morning it was, the traffic into Dulles wasn't too bad. Maj could almost have wished it was a little worse, in that there would have been more time for her to lose her bad mood completely. The reaction of the Group, when she had struck her head into Chel's workspace and announced that she couldn't stay for the meeting, was all too predictable, especially from those who had stayed up late. 'Look, I'll meet you all early here tonight,' Maj had said as she turned to go, and Shih Chin, usually so good-tempered, had actually growled, 'Miss Madeline, if you're late tonight . . . we're going without you. The battle starts at six central . . .'

'I know, I know, I won't be . . .' Maj had said, unnerved by the mutter of annoyance coming from the others. She had fled, then, intent on getting into the bathroom for at least a few minutes before she would have to get dressed and pile into the car with the rest of the crowd. Now here she sat, feeling rather hot and bothered, insufficiently showered, and altogether not caring whether she made any kind of good first impression on anybody.

Yet she was still distracted by the one connection she couldn't put together. *James Winters . . . and Dad. Talking about him.* Maj sighed. *I'm going to have to cut him some kind of slack, I guess, no matter how annoyed I am.*

The Muffin was oblivious to all this, and to everything else, as the car pulled out of the fast-speed 'lanes' and chimed at her father for him to take control back to do local approach. She was singing 'We have a cousin, we have a cousin!' at the top of her none-too-small lungs as Maj's dad slipped into the airport parking approach and brought the car around into the access circle, where once again the local remote control computers took it off his hands and guided it into the parking facility. Nothing was allowed to randomly circle within a kilometer from the airport center. There were too many things cycling through the neighborhood at the best of times to allow parking-place anarchy in, too.

'We're running early,' Maj's mother said, somewhat surprised, from the other front seat, as the car settled gently into the parking place that the local space-control had assigned it.

'Welcome to Dulles International Aerospace Port,' said a pleasant male voice through the car's entertainment system. 'To better serve our visitors, please note that parking rates in short-term are now thirty dollars per hour. Thank you for your cooperation in keeping our airport running smoothly.'

Her father grunted, a sound which Maj knew concealed a comment that would have been much more vigorous if the Muffin hadn't been in the car. 'Come on,' he said, 'let's get in there and fetch our guest before we have to go into escrow to get out again.'

A couple of rows from their space was the shelter for the maglev car that ran to the main terminals, and they all made their way to it, wincing a little at the sound of cars all around them parking or winding up their engines to take off again. Maj looked with some dry amusement at the poster inside the shelter as they climbed into the maglev car which almost immediately slid up to meet them – GROWING AGAIN TO SERVE YOU BETTER! This was Dulles's third 'refit' in the last twenty years, almost finished – so the airport kept promising – now that the fifth runway, the one for the aerospaceplanes, was finished, and the additional wing to Terminal C was almost done being extended and overhauled to service it. It wasn't entirely ready, though, and so it came to pass that the place where they met Niko looked more like a building site than a terminal.

And Maj, all too ready to be annoyed with him, caught the first sight of the youngster standing over near the 'designated meeting' area with the AA flight services lady, and immediately felt all her annoyance drop off her in embarrassment. It was impossible to be angry at anyone who looked so small and lost and scared, and who was trying so valiantly to hide it.

He really was kind of small for his age, his dark jeans and sober sweatshirt and plain dark jacket, like something left over from a school uniform, suggesting that he had somehow been trying to avoid notice, and indeed he looked uncomfortable, standing there out in the open, as if he would have preferred to be invisible.

Maj's dad made straight for him, and Maj hung back a little, watching the kid's face as he registered this tall, balding man heading in his direction, waiting to see his reaction. The boy looked at her father with dark, assessing eyes. He was himself shadowy – dark hair, a little bit olive of complexion, and had sort of a Mediterranean look, though with high cheekbones. As Maj's dad came up and paused there, towering over him, the slightest sign of a smile appeared, and it was a relieved smile.

'Martin Green,' her father said to the flight services lady. 'And this would be Niko. *Grazé*, cousin.'

'*Grazé* . . .' said the boy, as Maj and her mother and the Muffin came along behind her dad.

'Professor Green, can I get you to look into this, please?' said the flight services lady, holding up a 'little black box' with an eyepiece.

'No problem.' He took it from her, took off his driving glasses, and fitted the eyepiece to his eye. Then, 'Ow,' he said, and handed the box back. 'Can they make that light any brighter?'

The flight services lady laughed, turning the box over to check the LCD readout as it came up. 'Probably not. That's fine, Professor. Can I get you to sign this, please?' She held out an electric 'pad' and a stylus to him.

He scribbled his name, handed the pad back. 'Thanks, ma'am. Where's his luggage?'

'There wasn't any,' said the flight services lady, glancing down at Niko. 'Some kind of problem with the onload from the train at Zurich . . . The baggage people are trying to track it down. They have your number. They'll deliver it to your house as soon as it's found.'

'Oh, my gosh, that's awful,' said Maj's mother immediately. 'What an awful way to have a trip start! We'll sort something out for you. Welcome, Niko, I'm Rosilyn. And this is Madeline. Maj, we call her. And this is Adrienne—'

'I'm not Adrienne, I'm Muffin!' said the Muf in defiance, and then – apparently startled out of her wits by having actually spoken to her 'cousin' – the Muffin did the impossible, and came down with an acute case of the shys. She actually hid behind Maj's mother and looked around the side of her, as if she were a tree. 'Hi,' she whispered, and hid her face in Maj's mother's trousers.

Her mother and father looked at her in astonishment. Maj took the moment to hold her hand out. Niko reached out and shook it. 'Hello,' he said, and then looked up at her father and mother. 'Thanks for letting me stay with you.'

'No problem at all,' said Maj's father. 'Look, if your luggage is lost en route, there's no point in us standing around here trying to second-guess these people. Let's get home and have some breakfast. Or lunch, or dinner, or whatever your body clock us up for . . .'

They headed out of the torn-up terminal, past the posters with pictures of how it would look when it was finished, and Maj noticed that her father seemed to be rather more in a hurry than usual. Normally he liked poring over the details of new construction when they came across it. Then again, there was always the possibility that thirty dollars an hour for short-term parking was on his mind.

On their way back to the parking lot, Maj noticed how politely Niko seemed to be trying to pay attention to everything her mother and father said, while at the same time looking at absolutely everything around him as if he had never seen anything like it before. The Muffin was beginning to get over her shyness, and had made her way around her mother, while the maglev car was in transit, to sit closer to Niko. He had noticed this, and was smiling at her while he answered Maj's mom's questions about how things were in Hungary, the weather and so forth. By the time they got to the car, and started to get in, the Muffin had apparently decided that there was no further need for shyness, and insisted on being belted in beside Niko.

'I thought Hungry was something you got,' said the Muffin as the car lifted off.

Maj rolled her eyes in amusement, listening with one ear as Niko tried to explain the difference between a country and something that happened in your stomach. With the other ear she was amused to hear her mother going with unusual speed into full maternal mode.

'That's terrible about his clothes,' she said. 'And we haven't kept anything of Rick's that would fit him. And God knows when his luggage will arrive, or what continent it's on at this point. Never mind that. Maj, when we get in, why don't you take him over to GearOnline and pick up a few things for him? Jeans and so on. Put it on the house charge and we'll sort it out later.'

'Sure, Mom.' This raised some interesting questions for Maj, as she had never taken a boy clothes shopping before and wasn't sure if the online protocols were the same as they were for girls. Next to her, the Muffin's conversation was rapidly gaining in speed and volume as the car fed itself into the traffic stream heading back toward Alexandria. 'Our car is old,' the Muffin said, 'Mommy says it's an antique. It's a big car. Is your car like this one?'

59

Maj saw Niko's glance out of the window – a casual one, though his face seemed to her to be fixed in an expression of quiet amazement. 'Oh, no,' he said, and Maj caught just a flicker of amusement in his eyes as he turned away from the windows. 'We don't have cars where I come from.'

This news astonished the Muffin almost into silence, but she quickly recovered. 'What do you have?'

'We have cows,' Niko said, and he glanced at Maj just for a second as he said it, so that there was no mistaking the wicked humor. 'We ride them when we need to travel.'

Maj kept her face straight. The Muffin was hanging on every word he said, her mouth open, her eyes big and round. For his own part, Niko had eyes for none of the rest of them at the moment. 'And we ride them everywhere. Even to the airport.'

'They would poop in the road,' the Muffin said after a moment.

Niko looked at Maj again, his eyes eloquent of laughter being held under absolute control. ' "Poop"—'

'Uh, excrete,' Maj said. 'Defecate.'

'Absolutely they poop,' Niko said to the Muffin. 'But it doesn't matter, because we do not just ride the cows; we make them carry our things as well. The cows we ride have little carts behind them. And between the cows and the carts, we put canvas slides with buckets at the end, and the poop goes down the slides into the buckets.'

'What do you do with the buckets?' the Muffin whispered, absolutely riveted.

'Empty them over people's rosebushes,' Niko said.

'That's it,' said Maj's mother; 'you're moving in with us for at least a year. Someone who understands what rosebushes need is welcome in *our* house for as long as he cares to stay.'

They were only in transit for another fifteen minutes or so, but Maj found them some of the funniest fifteen minutes she had ever heard, as Niko kept spinning absurd stories about 'Hungry' for the Muffin. Her mother, though, once glanced back at her, and Maj found herself knowing exactly what her mother was thinking – that Niko's funniness had an edge to it, and somehow felt very purposeful – as if he was trying to distract himself.

And who knows, I might do the same thing, Maj thought. *Arriving in a strange country, meeting strangers, not even having my luggage with me . . . And,* something at the back of her mind added, *not having the slightest idea what was going to happen to me next . . .*

They landed at home, and the Muffin was practically the first one out, pulling on Niko's arm and demanding, 'Come and see my room!'

'He'll come in a while, honey,' Maj's mother said. 'Right now you have to have your breakfast.' The look she threw over her shoulder at Maj added, *And give this poor kid five minutes to breathe!*

'I'm not hungry!'

'Yes, you are,' Maj's mother said with serene certainty. 'Maj, honey, show Niko the guest room, and where the bathroom is . . .'

'Come on,' Maj said to him, and led him down the hallway, pushing the guest room door open. It had been her mother's office once before the 'new wing' had been built onto the end of the house several years back. Now it had a comfy old sofa in it, and a single bed, and a beat-up chest of drawers that had been in Rick's room, and bookshelves . . . lots of bookshelves, all full, mostly of 'overflow' books from her father's study. Niko looked around at it all. 'You read a lot,' he said, as if he approved.

'Not as much as I wish I had time to,' Maj said, and sighed a little. 'Here's the closet . . . not that you have anything to hang up in it at the minute! Look, take a few minutes to get yourself sorted out, and we'll go online and get you some clothes. Come on, here's the bathroom . . .'

She showed it to him, and Niko disappeared into it with a grateful look. Maj dodged into her dad's study, woke the Net machine up out of standby mode, and 'told' the implant chair there that it was going to have a new implant to add to its list of authorized users. When Niko appeared again, Maj pointed him at the chair and said, 'I'll access it from the kitchen and show you the way . . . we have a doubler in there. Sit yourself down, get comfortable . . .'

He sat down, wriggling a little as the chair got used to him and molded itself to his body. 'It's very strange,' he said. 'Mine does not do that . . .'

Maj grinned at him. 'For a moment there I thought you were going to tell me you sat on cows for this, too.'

He grinned back. After a moment he said, 'When does it start? I do not see anything.'

'Uh oh,' Maj said. 'Mom?'

Her mother appeared a moment later at the study door. 'Problems?'

'He should be in my workspace by now. But he's not getting anything.'

Her mother looked bemused. She came around to stand behind the chair in which Niko sat, and lined up her own implant with the Net computer, then blinked. 'It doesn't recognize his implant,' she said, and rolled her eyes. 'The story of my life. Why they can't just get everyone to agree to standardize these things . . .'

For a moment more Maj's mother stood still. 'Okay, I see,' she said then. 'It's just a different protocol . . . we don't use that one much over here. Let me just tell the machine what it should do instead . . .'

A moment's silence. 'Okay, Niko,' her mother said then. 'Try that and see how it works.'

He tilted his head a little to one side, then straightened it again. 'Oh!' he said.

'It's a jury-rig,' Maj's mother said, not sounding entirely happy. 'Your implant had a bandwidth limiter written into the code. I just circumvented it. It can be put back the way it was whenever you like. Are the visuals OK now?'

'*Yes . . .!*'

'Okay. Maj, check the sales area. It's getting to be the time of year when they'll be reducing prices on some of the spring boys' wear . . . and this is just for casual wear anyway. Niko doesn't have to worry about being a fashion plate at the moment. His luggage will be here in a while anyway. If you want to use the machine in my office, go ahead, I won't need it for an hour or so . . .'

'Okay, Mom, thanks. Stay there, Niko, I'll be with you in a minute . . .'

She went around to her mom's office and settled into the chair there. A moment later she was in her workspace, and Niko was standing there, looking around him in astonishment. 'This is . . . very sophisticated,' he said after a moment.

'A poor thing, but mine own,' said Maj. 'Computer . . .'

'Yes, boss?' said her workspace.

'GearOnline, please. Boys' wear.'

'Enter, please.'

'Through here, Niko,' Maj said, and opened the door at the back of her workspace, between the bookshelves. Niko went over to it, peered through.

'*Bozhe moi,*' he said softly.

'I know,' Maj said. They walked through the door together. 'I don't shop here a lot any more. It's too easy to get confused . . .'

The sheer 'acreage' of the place always bewildered her a little; the designers had apparently decided to make this space a direct virtual descendant of the old snail-mail catalogs from the distant past, so that every single thing the chain stocked was out here, arranged on a 'floor' which Maj guessed was probably roughly equivalent to the area of the surface of the moon.

'Come on over here,' she said, and led him over to what looked like a single changing room, standing there by itself in the middle of the vast floor full of clothes hanging up on racks and stacked up folded on shelves. 'I don't see why we should wander around in all this and get lost. See this grid?' Maj pointed to a lighted square on the floor, all crisscrossed with grid lines. 'Just stand here . . .'

Niko stepped onto it, bemused. 'Store computer, please . . .'

'Ready to be of service, ma'am. And thank you for shopping GearOnline!'

'Yeah, sure. Please do a measurement template for this gentleman. Niko, hold still, the thing'll get confused if you twitch.'

The grid of light-lines peeled itself up off the 'floor' and wrapped itself around Niko, molding itself to him. He held quite still, but Maj could understand his slightly alarmed look – the template's feel could be rather snug.

'Don't freak. It's getting the readings off the sensors in the chair,' Maj said. 'By the way, that was great, in the car . . . the story you were telling the Muffin, about the cows.'

He gave her a slightly rueful look. 'You mean you don't believe it, then.'

'That you ride cows to work?' She had to laugh. 'Have you ever ridden a cow?'

He laughed, too, then. 'They are bony.'

'And they dump you off and step on you,' Maj said. 'I tried it once when I was little and my folks took me to a farm. Once was enough. Riding horses, though, that's another matter.'

'You ride—' There was a pause while he got rid of one set of gridwork, tried on another. 'Funny.'

Her eyebrows went up. 'Why would it be funny?'

'Oh. Your name.' Maj blinked. 'In my language, "Maj" might be short for "amajzona". Amazon. A woman who rides.'

She grinned a little. 'Well,' Maj said, 'the name is really Madeline, but we don't use it much.'

'A little cake? I think "amazon" is better—'

The grid of light walked off Niko and stood to one side, a Niko-shaped webwork, glowing green. Niko brushed himself down and stared at it. 'Now what do we do?'

'Go crazy trying to figure out what we want,' Maj said. 'Chair, please.'

A chair appeared. She sat down. 'You want to sit?' Maj said.

'Uh, no, it's all right,' Niko said. 'I was sitting a long time today.'

'Okay. Store program,' Maj said.

'Ready to be of service, ma'am, and—'

'Boy, I wish it wouldn't do that . . . What kinds of things do you want to wear, Niko?'

'Uh – jeans would be fine. Maybe a shirt.'

'Jeans,' Maj said. Instantly a pair of them appeared on the wireframe model of Niko. 'How do they look?'

He walked around the model. 'And these will fit—'

'Real closely. The company will pull the closest match off the rack in the warehouse and van them over. They have a delivery run out this way a few times a day.'

'Do they have to be blue?' he said.

'You want a different color?'

'Uh . . .' He smiled, a very small shy smile. 'I always wanted black ones.'

'Black, absolutely,' said Maj, and the color of the jeans on the wireframe figure changed. She grinned at him. 'Black's back in this year. Want the shirt that color, too? It'll look good on you.'

'Yes!'

The heck with the sale stuff. 'Formshirt, black,' said Maj. One of the tight-fitting shirts that were coming in right now appeared on the wireframe. 'How about that?'

His smile said it all.

'Great,' said Maj. 'Store program/ Select both, purchase both.'

'Account confirmation.'

'Eighteen twelve,' Maj said.

'Thank you. Pick up or send?'

'Send.'

'Thank you. Your purchases will be dispatched from our Bethesda warehouse at ten a.m.'

'That's it,' Maj said, and got up. 'Can you think of anything else you need?'

'Anything . . .' Niko looked out across that huge space of clothes, across which Maj sometimes thought one should be able to see the curvature of the earth. 'No,' Niko said, and sounded shy again. 'But thank you.'

She patted him on the shoulder. He jumped a little, as if taken by surprise. 'It's okay,' Maj said. 'Come on, let's climb out of here, my mom's going to want her machine back.'

'It is . . . a Sunday? And still your mother works?'

Maj rolled her eyes. 'It's more like no one can stop her working. Come on . . .'

'And thank you for shopping at—' the system shouted after them, rather desperately, as they deactivated their implants. Maj snickered as the two of them headed back into the kitchen. 'Are you hungry?' Maj said.

'Uh . . .' He paused to look out the window at the back yard, which Maj's mother's tomatoes and rosebushes were threatening to take over, just as they always did this time of year. 'Something to drink, maybe.'

'Tea? Milk? Coffee?'

Niko didn't answer. He was leaning against the window-sill, apparently lost in thought. 'Niko?' Maj said.

No response.

'Niko?!'

He jumped as if he had been shot, and turned around in a hurry. 'Uh, sorry, yes . . .'

'Do you want some tea, or coffee, or—'

He stared at her . . . then relaxed, all over, so obvious a gesture that it practically shouted, *I thought you were going to do something terrible to me . . . but it's all right now.* 'Um,' he said then. 'Coffee, that would be good.'

'How do you like it?'

'A lot of milk.'

'Fine. We'll steal Mom's coffee – it's the best in the house.' She got out one of her mother's single-pack drip coffee containers, put it on a mug, put the kettle on, and went to the fridge, opening it and rummaging around. 'Let's see – oh, here it is.' She pulled out a quart of milk past the door scanner.

'That's the last liter,' said the fridge. 'Do you want more?'

'Jeez,' Maj muttered, 'the way we go through this stuff. My brother must just pour it over his—' As she turned, she saw that Niko was staring at the fridge, completely stunned.

'Your refrigerator *talks?*' he said.

Maj blinked at that. 'Oh. Yeah. Mostly to complain.' She made an amused face, pulled the door open to show him the little glass plate set in it. 'See, there's a scanner here, you run everything in front of it when you put things in after you go shopping. It keeps track of everything by the bar codes, and then when you run out, it orders more. It has a little Net connection inside, and it calls the grocery store. The delivery van comes around in the mornings and replaces what you've used up.' She shook the liter carton, made a face. 'It may not be soon enough, the way my brother drinks this stuff.' She turned back to the door, waved the carton in front of it again.

'Ordering more,' said the refrigerator.

Maj closed the door. 'The new ones don't even ask,' she said, 'they just do it – they estimate your needs and update their own order lists. This one's kind of an antique, but there's something about the door handles my mother likes, and she won't get rid of it.'

Niko sat down with a wry look. 'Our refrigerators aren't . . . quite so talkative.'

'Believe me, it might not be a bad thing,' Maj said, sitting down across the table. 'This one's always bugging me about using too much butter. My brother keeps enabling the "dietary advice" function just to annoy me, and I have to keep turning it off.' She made a face.

The kettle, which her mother must just have boiled, shrieked with very little waiting time. Maj poured the coffee first, then the tea, so they would come out together, then put them both on the table. Niko was already sitting down there.

'Niko—' she said.

This time there was something almost deliberate about the way he responded. 'Yes.'

'You look completely wrecked,' Maj said.

He stared at her . . . and his face sagged, as if being confronted with his own weariness made it all right to reveal it. 'Yes,' he said. 'Tired, you mean?'

'Tired, yes. Wasted. Utterly paved. Do you want to take a nap? Get some rest, I mean?'

'For a while,' he said, 'I would not mind.'

'Have your coffee, first. There's no rush. You're—' She stopped herself, for her intention had been to say, *You're safe here.* Then she realized that she had no idea why she was going to say it. Except that he had been carrying himself very much like someone who was not safe, someone who was seriously afraid.

Time to get this sorted out, Maj thought.

'You're among family,' she said. 'You don't have to sit up and be polite around us. You're jetlagged, you look like you could use some rest. You rest as much as you want. When you feel like getting up, get up. Maybe later this evening. I have some Net stuff to do . . . if you want to come along, you'd be welcome.'

I can't believe I'm saying this, she thought. *But he needs a friend right now, poor kid . . . and virtuality is one thing, but reality is another. Reality takes precedence.*

At the mention of the Net, his eyes lit up. 'I would like that,' he said. 'Very much!'

'Yeah,' Maj said. 'Look, take your coffee with you . . . go on, get your rest. I'll wake you up around five, and you can come see what I'm up to. It's pretty neat.'

He nodded and got up with his coffee cup. 'It was the fourth room down?'

'Fourth room down. If the Muffin tries to bother you, just throw her out.'

'She would not bother me,' he said, and grinned briefly, and just for the moment looked much less tired. 'She is very – cute?'

'Cute. You got that right,' Maj said. 'Welcome to America, kiddo. Go get some sleep.'

He vanished down the hall. Maj waited about fifteen minutes, and then went to find her father.

Three

Major Arni would really have preferred to handle this meeting as a phone call, or virtually. But she could not, for Ernd Bioru outranked her considerably – not in straightforward military rank, which she could have dealt with, but in the shadowy and uncomfortable outranking which a very few politicians held over her department – and if he demanded an in-person meeting, he would expect his request, or rather order, to be dealt with instantly.

She stood there in the big plush office full of expensive furniture and watercolors waiting for Bioru to look up, and fumed at being treated like a piece of furniture herself. Unfortunately there was nothing she could do about it. The Minister for Internal Defense had Cluj's ear, and a whisper in that particular appendage could land you in all kinds of uncomfortable or permanent places if you weren't careful. Inwardly, she scorned Bioru, for he had opted out of the working ranks of the intelligence service early, choosing instead to go abroad on diplomatic duties – achieving status by subtle means rather than by the overt hard work and slow climb through the ranks which the Major considered the approved manner. Outwardly, though, she kept her manner towards Bioru correct and a touch subservient. It was safer to do so at the moment. In a year, two years, five, things might change, and an officer who had kept her mouth shut and done her work properly might yet see this upstart thrown out on his own ear. Cluj was well known in the upper reaches of government to be a volatile man, and even those who thought they best knew his mind and could 'manage' him had received some savage surprises, just in these last few years. But for now—

Now she looked at this short, slight, dark little man in his fancy charcoal-gray foreign suit, and cursed him in her mind as he sat there reading his paperwork, page by deliberate page, and not looking up, just making her stand there. Finally he put the papers aside and sat back in his big comfortable chair, and looked at her. His was one of those bland faces, for all the sharpness of the bone structure. There was no telling what was going on inside that smooth regard – approval or rage – and no way to anticipate which way he would jump. That immobile face made the blue eyes look curiously flat, like a shark's.

For all his diplomatic service, there was nothing of the diplomat about Bioru at the moment. 'Major,' he said, 'where is the boy?'

'Sir, he is in a private home in the Alexandria area. As far as we can tell, the man holding him is an old scholastic associate of the father.'

He drummed his fingers on the expensive desk. ' "As far as you can tell"?' he said. 'This kind of vagueness sits oddly with your reputation for precision and effectiveness, Major.'

'Unfortunately the spaceplane was diverted due to a mechanical fault,' Major Arni said, wondering one more time exactly how likely that was with a machine as carefully serviced as spaceplanes were, especially the hybrids. 'Our operative had been at Baltimore-Washington, and we were unable to get an operative to Dulles in time to do a more effective intercept. Not that the security systems in operation would have made a straight lift of the boy possible at that time.'

'Considering the case in hand, you should have had someone at all that area's airports.'

'Budget limitations do not permit us such latitude, sir,' she said. 'I am sorry.'

There it was, she had had to say it. Now all she could do was wonder how he would take it.

To the Major's amazement, Bioru let it pass. 'As long as you know where the boy is now.'

'We were able to determine that immediately from the local traffic computers,' the Major said, 'to which the DC area police have access. Fortunately we have a source in the police force. Such personnel are chronically under-paid, and usually do not look carefully at where their data goes after they allow it to be leaked.'

He nodded at that, turned over another page. 'Just in a private house, though, you say.'

'Yes, sir. In the suburbs. We are running a background check on the father at the moment. There are some connections which are not immediately analyzable, but that is understandable, when a background in political science is involved. The mother and the rest of the family are of no interest.'

'You have someone doing surveillance at the house now?'

'Yes, sir.'

'Is it someone you trust?'

She swallowed. 'For the moment.'

Bioru looked up sharply, held her gaze for a moment. 'Surely you're not angling for an assignment over there for *yourself*,' he said.

'I have the language skills, granted,' said the Major, 'but I have more pressing matters occupying me here.'

'Such as?'

She knew an incoming rebuke when she saw it, and understood the message that nothing was more important than *this* was at the moment, at least to this man. 'Sir,' she said, 'I am entirely at your disposal in this regard.' Then she immediately became sorry she had used the word 'disposal.'

'Huh,' Bioru said, a noncommittal sound, and turned his attention back to his papers, turned a couple of them over. 'It says here that work has begun on questioning the father's immediate associates,' he said. ' "Equivocal results", it says here.'

'The associates are—'

'One of them is *dead*,' Bioru said. 'I would not normally call that "equivocal." What kind of bunglers are you employing over there?'

'Sir, we can be as conscientious as anyone would wish—'

'Not so much so as *I* would wish, plainly.'

'—but we can hardly be held responsible for physiological reactions toward which the subject has never previously shown any tendency. The woman who died had no history of any kind of cardiac difficulty; she had undergone the usual pre-questioning workup to rule out anything that might interfere. Her cardiac arrest was attended by the University doctors, and they confirmed that such things happen sometimes without any clear reason—'

'Except pain,' Bioru said dryly. 'You overdid it. Or your "technician" did. I want that person removed to other duties. No one is to work on this project except the most senior tech we have who's qualified for this work.'

She swallowed. 'Sir, it *was* the most senior tech who was involved.'

He stared at her for a long moment . . . then pulled the paperwork over again and let out a breath. 'Nothing was yet proven against that woman when she died,' he said, looking down and paging through it. 'That leaves us in an unpleasant moral situation. I should make him pay compensation to the family out of his own salary.' Bioru sighed. 'All right . . . let him stay. But I want his junior technician to work with him closely and monitor all his intervention choices. If he catches his boss in a mistake, well, we save another of these poor creatures for further investigation, and the underling gets a promotion.'

'Yes, sir.' The Major had no quarrel with that method of operation. It was what she had used to get into her present position.

'So on to more urgent matters. The father—'

'Is still missing,' she said. 'But the search continues. The scientists with whom he routinely socializes at the University have been as cooperative as their personal loyalties allow.' She got another sharp look for that. 'Sir,' she said, 'if they are to remain of any use to us as scientists, we must take some care not to overly alienate them. They do understand our security concerns—'

'They had better,' Bioru growled. 'Those are more important than the whole pack of them. They'd better come to understand that. Better have some friendly source whisper that news in their ears before we have to make examples of a few more of them. Your dead one here – an accident she may have been, but maybe she'll speed the process up a little . . . get the rest of them thinking harder about letting us know exactly where Darenko might have thought to hide himself away. A chance word could make the difference between finding him quickly, or taking forever about it and looking incompetent. See to it.' He pushed the papers away again. 'Meanwhile, what news on the search?'

'Nothing new, sir. He does not seem to be in the city.'

He pushed himself back in his chair and gave her a look of extreme annoyance. 'It's not as if he'll have managed to get across the border,' he said. 'He's in-country *somewhere*. Have the usual statements gone out to the press?'

'Yes, sir.' Privately the Major had her doubts about the effectiveness of these CITIZENS! HELP YOUR LEADER! announcements. Most citizens didn't have the brains to find their own fundaments with a flashlight and a road map, and the rest could be surprisingly obstructive at times, even in the extreme cases when rewards were offered. Hoax responses to these announcements abounded, usually leaving you with more people to discipline and no useful results.

'Find him,' Bioru said. 'Find him immediately. That's all I want from you in that regard. Go door-to-door, use dogs, use infrared, use molecular air-sampling, use whatever you have to. I want him hunted down like a murderer. Are you clear how urgent this is? The President himself has asked to be briefed about this proceeding. And the performance of the personnel associated with it.'

The sweat broke out all over her, instantly, and she hoped desperately that it wouldn't show. 'Yes, sir,' the Major said, and hoped her voice betrayed nothing of what she was feeling.

Those eyes went back to looking flat again, much to the Major's relief. 'We have some other technicians,' Bioru said then, a little more calmly, 'going through the extant data from the project at the moment. This could be very,

very lucrative stuff . . . very useful. Most specifically, there are intelligence implications for us once we get the technique working and in production. The ability to carry the longest message undetectably, swimming free in a courier's blood, assembling itself into content only on command . . . or the ability to take a rogue operative's brain apart from the inside in a matter of hours. The little things eat holes all through it and leave it looking like a Swiss cheese. The results look just like, what was it called, mad cow disease.' He smiled a little at the image. 'Even the North Americans have nothing like these little–' he lifted one of the pages, glanced down at it '–microps. And we intend to make sure it stays that way.'

He looked up at her. 'The boy,' he said. 'Preparations must be made to have him recovered, without fuss, *on signal* and not a moment before or later . . . for we'll need him to work on the father. I'll give you details when you need them. Take the minimum of time to assess the situation and then get him out of there and back over here. You might want to exit the country in the opposite direction, toward the Far East. They might not immediately expect that. Or the great-circle route over Canada. If you feel the need, go yourself,' he said. 'I'll authorize the expense immediately. But his recovery must be so managed as to happen *before* the father's found, if what we're planning is to have the maximum effect. His own interrogation is going to require that the part of it involving the boy be very precisely timed . . . otherwise the father will have no incentive to cooperate properly with us.' Bioru frowned. 'He's one of those stubborn ones as it is, a psych profile like a rock . . . the break-but-don't-bend type. A nuisance, likely to kill himself to keep us from finding out what we need. However, if the boy's situation has been made properly threatening . . . if the timing is right . . . he'll not only not suicide, but he'll help us gladly, and beg to be allowed to do so for as long as we like.'

Bioru smiled, and suddenly she realized why he had been taken out of the diplomatic service and redirected into politics. No diplomat, seeing that expression across a desk from him, seeing those eyes come alive, would do anything but panic. 'Get on it,' he said. 'I want you in place to make the recovery on signal. There are some aspects of the operation that have to be finessed at our end before it can go ahead. For the time being, close surveillance will do. I will be in contact with you immediately you arrive over there, in the usual way. Make sure you're ready to jump the instant you hear from me.'

From me. Not from her normal superiors. *How many levels above me have been cut out of this operation?* The Major thought. *Or perhaps cut out permanently?*

'Yes, sir,' she said, saluted, and left, resolved to carry this whole business out with absolute care and panache. There could be all kinds of promotions at the end of it, if everything worked out.

There would certainly be all kinds of shootings, if it didn't.

He was nowhere to be found when she went looking for him; at least nowhere in the house where Maj would go – there being an understanding that the children of the family did not enter their parents' bedroom without permission, or knock on the door when it was shut except in the case of emergency or a phone or link call that hadn't been picked up. That door was shut, and Maj looked at it, shrugged, then went back into the kitchen to see if there was any more e-mail, and look over the Group of Seven briefing again.

There was nothing new in her in-box – or rather the slick steel-and-hardwood table where such things arrived in her workspace – and the briefing told her nothing she hadn't digested the first time around. *We're going to have a bad time of it,* was most of what she had learned from the first reading. A big amateur squadron had gone in last night in a pre-emptive attack on the space station which was the focus of this operation, trying to snatch a little glory for themselves. They had managed to just get away with their skins, and not much more. The defenses of the place were redoubtable, and the Archon's forces had been waiting for them, not even a particularly large grouping of the Black Arrows . . . but it had shredded poor Dawn-Squad, 'killing' most of the players and leaving the rest of them with crippled ships. Maj was feeling increasingly nervous at having missed the briefing and the final practice session which followed it. Nothing to do about it now . . . she thought. *Just go in there tonight, tough it out, do our best . . .*

. . . As DawnSquad had done its best. The thought nagged at her as she got up and stretched. She listened to the air around her. Somewhere in the distance she thought she could hear Mom and the Muffin talking together, the Muf still all excited, her mother making sedate calm-down-dear noises as she worked. She was in the household Net, probably working online, and keeping the Muffin occupied and away from Niko's bedroom at the same time. *Quite an accomplishment . . .* Maj thought.

'Dad?' she said to the air.

There was a pause. 'Yeah, hon?'

'You busy?'

'In my office.'

She smiled slightly. 'The big one or the little one?'

79

'Both.'

'Got a moment?'

'Sure.'

Maj went to the door in her back wall, opened it, stepped through.

Books, and the echo – that was always her first impression. Her father was one of those people who read every hour of the day, who read anything, and then filed the information away in their heads, seemingly able to find it again at a moment's notice years later. She wondered sometimes whether this library was a conscious expression of that trait, a joke, or just good old fashioned virtual wish-fulfilment, his picture of where he'd like to be if he had his choice. Now, as she walked down the long, long hall full of brown shelves full of books, towering up toward the ceiling, reaching away in all directions, she found herself leaning toward the latter theory. And it made her smile, for her father couldn't make up his mind where he wanted to be.

There was part of this place, about a half a mile along the central hall, which looked like a straightforward reconstruction of the Great Library of Alexandria, burned along with all its books three thousand years ago – open porticoes and columns, that ruthless Mediterranean sun blazing outside, the sea lapping up nearly against the steps. The area to which she was now coming looked more like the old British Museum Reading Room – a high, light dome, a huge circular room full of shelves and ladders for climbing up without killing yourself. But out one of the side doors, Maj knew, was a part that looked more like the National Library in Dublin, all carved mahogany shelves with busts of philosophers on pedestals and the Book of Kells in a glass case down at one end.

Another hallway favored the Stiftsbibliotek in St Gallen in Switzerland – thousands of shelves in light wood, aged dark, high stained-glass windows half a millennium old, a floor worn smooth by twenty lifetimes' worth of readers. A third one led out the front hall of the New York Public Library and left you standing on the stairs between the two white lions, Patience and Fortitude. 'I always have a soft spot for that one,' her dad had told her once. 'They threw me out of there once when I was six . . .'

She kept meaning to ask him what he'd done. But for the moment there was other business. She wandered through into the light streaming down through the dusty air from the windows set high in the dome of the Reading Room, and made her way over to where her father's desk sat incongruously in the middle of it all. He looked up as she came over.

All those Eastern European books and magazines were still scattered over the desk. He pushed a few of them off to one side to make room for Maj to sit down. 'Quiet out there,' he said.

'For the moment,' Maj said. 'Mom has the Muffin. Niko's had a collapse.'

Her dad raised his eyebrows. 'Nothing serious, I hope!'

'No,' she said as she swung herself up onto the desk and got comfortable. 'Just jet lag, I think. But, Daddy,' Maj said, 'his name's not Niko.'

Her father turned a rather shocked expression on her. 'What did he—?'

'He didn't tell me anything,' Maj said. Then she smiled slightly. 'He doesn't *answer* to it, that's all. Not the first time, anyway.'

'Oh,' her father said. 'Oh . . .' He sighed. 'Well, this was why I wanted to talk to you, anyway. What is it with the timing of things, this weekend? Everything keeps getting messed up . . .'

She idly picked up one of the bound sets of Eastern European magazines. 'He's not really a relative of ours, is he?' she said.

Her father shook his head. 'Not by blood.'

'So what was that big story you told us yesterday?'

'I knew you were going to pick up on that,' he said, looking rueful. 'I would have preferred to tell you and your Mom right then, but the Muffin was there . . . and if she didn't think she had an immediate handle on who our guest was, she would have started asking questions. And probably in public as well as in private. The fewer questions asked about our guest, the better.'

Maj was inclined to agree. The Muffin had the family curiosity in full measure, and if she thought someone had a secret, she would pester them mercilessly. For her, all secrets smacked of Christmas or birthdays. 'Simpler to let her think he's what his ID says, I guess.'

'I thought so. But truly, Maj, I didn't want you to think I didn't trust you. It was all just bad timing.'

Maj nodded. 'Daddy, it's OK. You told Mom, didn't you?'

'Last night.'

'I think she tried to tell me this morning. Just bad timing again. The Muffin arrived in the middle of it. So what *is* he really?'

'A thirteen-year-old kid,' her father said, running one hand wearily through what was left of his hair, 'whose father is very big in biotech in his home country. Which is the Calmani Republic.'

Maj had to search around in her head for a moment to think why the name seemed familiar. 'It was part of

Romania, wasn't it?' Maj said. 'It split up.'

'Sort of the same situation as Carpathia,' her father said. 'Worse, in a way . . . from the historian's point of view, anyway. Never mind that. His dad has been working on some cutting-edge research in biotech. Stuff that would be advanced even if it were being done on our side of the cultural divide. Nanotechnics . . .'

'Microsurgery,' Maj said, 'that kind of thing?'

'More involved,' her father said. 'I don't understand the details. Frankly, I don't think a *lot* of people are equipped to understand the details . . . which is probably the source of the trouble. He's really one of the brilliant ones, a groundbreaking scientist in his particular art. Which is building the smallest machines anyone's ever seen, and programming them to do the most delicate work possible . . . at the molecular level, maybe even the atomic level.'

He folded his arms and looked thoughtful for a moment. 'He and I met at Georgetown together when I was doing my master's. One of those unusual friendships – heaven knows, "interdisciplinary" stuff is considered strange enough on campus. When a physicist or a biologist starts to hang around with Humanities people, there are those who'll start to question the sanity of both sides. And there was the language barrier as well. And even beyond that, a certain amount of mistrust. Everybody knew why his government had sent him over, and Armin wasn't too sure at first that we weren't all spies. But despite everything, Armin and I hit it right off. And he amazed me from the very beginning. I knew he was going to be big at whatever he decided to do.'

Her father stretched, then smiled a little. 'You know this thing, that your mom likes to do when you complain?' He

83

lifted one hand, rubbed the thumb and forefinger together. ' "This is the world's smallest violin, and it's playing just for you?" '

Maj laughed, and her father looked ironic, for the truth was that mostly her mother used that gesture on *him*. 'Well, once, as a joke, when he had met your mother – this was some time before we were married – and heard her use that line on me, he *built* that. The world's smallest violin. Four longchain molecules fastened together with benzene rings, and one molecule knitted back into itself for a bow. Five thin little hyoprotein constructs for strings on the violin. One to string the bow. And a tiny submolecular wheel and pulley to make the bow go back and forth across the string. I saw it work. Of course, you needed an electron microscope to see it.' He grinned.

'He did that as a *joke?*'

Her father nodded, somber. 'That was always the problem with Armin,' he said. 'You never knew what to say around him, because you might give him an idea for something he could build . . . and then he would vanish for weeks at a time until it was done. Oh, he'd come out for exams and lectures and so on . . . but in between times, you wouldn't see him until he'd succeeded at what he was doing.' He sighed. 'Absolutely brilliant man. And with the most important part of brilliance – persistence.'

He let out a long breath. 'And now,' he said, 'I can't get in touch with him. Which, if it means what I'm afraid it means, suggests that what *he* was afraid was about to happen, has happened. They've arrested him.'

'Oh, Daddy, no!'

Her father nodded, looking grim. 'Maj, I don't know for sure. But he had hoped to be at his new contact address by now, so he told me the other day . . . so one way or another, something's gone wrong. I really hope they don't have him. It would be bad news if they did. But it's so soon, maybe too soon, to tell . . .'

He leaned back and looked across the room at nothing in particular. 'He saw this coming some time ago,' he said softly. 'Armin has been . . . well, maybe a little too brilliant. The Calmani government has been very much shut out of trade, the way Carpathia has. Import sanctions linked to improvement of their human-rights record – and since they have no intention of improving that, there are all kinds of things they can't get. High-technology things, mostly. To have someone like Armin was a big coup for them – someone who they could, in a way, use as a bargaining chip with the West. You want our technology, you have to trade us things *we* want.'

Her father raised his eyebrows. 'That by itself, maybe, didn't bother him. He loved his country, though I doubt he would have extended that love to his government. But Armin rarely stopped to think about such matters. He wanted to get busy creating things, and he was willing to stay where he had been born and do that . . . help his people, work for them, especially when he thought the Calmani government would help him do that. And for a while, he thought he was doing all right, and that the work he was doing would actually get to the people he was trying to help. But then I think he started to realize that the government had other plans for what he was doing. Especially the medical end of it. He was involved mostly with building micromechanisms that would heal people. The government, I suspect, saw them in an entirely different light. I don't know the details . . . but that was when Armin decided to defect. He was intent on getting Laurent – that's Niko's real name – out of there. Well,

85

that's gone well enough. Except that now the government certainly knows what he intends by what he's done.'

'Oh, no . . .' Maj swallowed.

Her father shook his head. 'Exactly what the problem is at the moment, what it is that made Armin decide to jump right now, I can't say. He wasn't willing to discuss it much, and I wasn't willing to press him on the subject. He was none too sure of how secure his own communications were; even the last one I got came to me second hand. But I think he had come up against some kind of crunch. Either he felt that he couldn't go on with his work as he had been . . . or that it was becoming too dangerous somehow . . . He was very oblique.'

Maj was still stuck with the idea that Niko's, no, Laurent's father was in some little windowless cell somewhere, with secret police looming over him. She imagined how she would feel in Laurent's place, and shivered. 'If they do have him . . . then what?'

'I wouldn't necessarily think that would be a permanent situation,' her father said. 'Armin has a lot of friends working for him, there . . . and here. Though "here" may matter more at the moment. Net Force is interested, as you'll doubtless be hearing. I spoke to James Winters this morning. It was the least I could do.'

Maj blushed hot, and slipped down off the desk to look at a book in a nearby bookshelf, for no reason except to keep her dad from seeing the look. 'You think they can get him out?' she said.

'If they can't, they can at least work out who to contact who can actually do the job. Net Force is owed all kinds of favors, all around the world, in some unlikely places.'

Maj wondered if this would be enough. 'That's a help, anyway.'

'Yes. But there are other things on my mind.' That worried note was in his voice again, and it made Maj's head turn. 'The Calmani authorities are hardly going to just sit around and let this happen without acting, honey. That's not their style. They're going to do their best to alter this situation to their liking. One good way to put pressure on Armin to do whatever it is they're trying to get him to do would be to threaten Laurent.'

'But he's here,' Maj said. 'What can they—'

Then she stopped. This house was not exactly a security zone. It was an ordinary suburban house with ordinary suburban locks on the doors and windows, and an ordinary security system mostly designed for stopping burglars, not kidnappers. If armed people came along and tried to snatch someone who was living here— She opened her mouth to say, 'The police—' and then stopped herself again. The police here were good . . . but were they good enough to take on armed snatch operatives? Or fast enough?

'We have a little security that doesn't show,' said her father. 'And more to be added shortly, at least of the "passive" kind. Some guys will be coming from "the phone company" to install it over the next day or so, so don't be surprised.' He ran one hand over where his hair used to be. 'It's a happy coincidence that I asked a month ago to have our lines checked for bandwidth constriction. This will look like that's being fixed, to the casual observer . . . but as a result, people on our side will be watching the house and its environs a little more closely than would otherwise be the case, until Laurent's dad makes it out safely.'

Maj nodded. 'Okay,' she said. 'I assume part of my job in this is to keep an eye on him.'

Her father nodded. 'You can't do much during school, I know that, but Mom will be working from home during the business week for the next little while, and she'll be able to keep watch during the day. If you could just stay with him during his recreation time, that'll be a help.'

'Does he have to stay inside?'

'Oh, no. Though he may need a little coaching in how to act when he goes out. He's not a dumb kid. He'll catch on quickly.'

Maj knew that already. 'Though,' her father said, 'you might want to keep an eye on what he's up to online, as well. His father was concerned about that.'

'What? About him being in the Net?'

'Yes.'

'But they have it, too . . .'

'Not as wide-bandwidth as ours,' her dad said, 'and there's not nearly as much for anyone to do. Their country's Net is more or less quarantined from the rest of the worldwide Net . . . and the quarantine has run both ways. They can't get their hands on the equipment they'd like to have. They've been embargoed for years. And from their side of things, they don't want their own people getting their hands on the kind of decadent liberal entertainment – not to mention news – that's available everywhere else in the world. So our Net is going to look pretty interesting to Laurent. His father sounded concerned about it, asked me very pointedly not to let his son overdo it, or even spend that much time on it, until he was available to help guide him through all the content.'

Maj nodded. 'I'll make sure he doesn't spend all day and all night on it,' she said. 'I can imagine it would be easy to get sucked into overdoing it.'

Her father nodded, ran his hand over his thin spot

again. 'At the same time,' he said, 'if you want to take him places where you can let him have some harmless entertainment . . .'

'No problem with that,' Maj said, and grinned. 'I had some plans for one of the places tonight.'

'Simming again?'

'Yes, but somebody else's sim,' Maj said. 'The Group have gotten into it in a big way. We have a battle scheduled this evening.'

'Well, if you want to take Laurent along, he'd probably thank you,' Her father sighed, rubbed his head again where his hair used to be.

'Daddy,' Maj said suddenly, 'I have to ask you. Please don't be mad. But *why don't you go have that grown back??*'

He looked at her, and then smiled. 'Honey,' he said, 'a lot of my "bosses" were born, oh, no later than the middle of the last century. They still have that century's values . . . though reminding them openly of that can be dangerous. Think about it. From their point of view, without being thin on top and looking elderly and respectable, how am I supposed to look like I deserve my tenure?'

He smiled a most ironic smile, then got up, squeezing her shoulder as he went by, and headed off among the shelves before Maj could think of anything to say.

She looked after him with a ghost of that smile, and then turned and made her way back to the door into her workspace.

Four

About half an hour later she ran into her mother in the kitchen. Her mother was looking frazzled. Plainly she had had a difficult morning on the machine. 'Any improvement?' Maj said.

'In their system? Some,' her mom said, leaning against the window, more or less as Laurent had, and looking out at the tomatoes. 'I've got to get out there and pinch those things back,' she said, 'or there are going to be eight hundred thousand tomatoes again this August. And I've made all the green tomato chutney I can stand.' She glanced down the hallway. 'Don't knock on his door, Muffin mine,' she said quickly. 'He's still sleeping.'

'I was just going to look,' said the plaintive little voice from down the hall.

'I know, sweetieMuf. *Don't*. Just go down and read to your dinosaurs now.'

'They're tired of reading.'

'Then tell them all about Niko's cows, the ones with the buckets.'

'*Oh*,' said the Muffin, delighted, and ran off down the hall. Her room door shut.

Maj's mother smiled. 'She's fascinated with him,' she said. 'For which he'll probably start being sorry when he wakes up. How is he, do you think?'

'Tired. And there's the other stuff going on.'

'Yes, his father . . . Daddy told you?'

'We had a word.'

'Yes.' Her mother looked suddenly more weary than she had. 'I feel for him, poor kid, being thrown out into the world all alone like this all of a sudden . . .I don't think there's any luggage coming, either. It seems that was just a "phantom record" generated by whoever sent him, to keep him from looking abnormal. Nobody but a government courier gets on a spaceplane without any bags, and I think poor Laurent must just have been hustled straight out of the country without any, on the grounds that anyone *with* luggage would attract suspicion . . .'

'Yeah,' Maj said. 'Well, his stuff came in from the warehouse . . . it's there on the counter. But, Mom, should I send for some more stuff for him? He's going to need more than just one pair of pants and jeans. GearOnline has his template.'

Her mother nodded. 'Sure, honey, that's a good idea. You take care of it.' She gave Maj a cautionary look. 'Try not to break the bank.'

'I won't.'

Her mother looked out the window again. 'I should get back to hammering on that system. But I've got to take a moment to do something about the aphids out there. Otherwise those nasty little suckers are going to pull those roses up by the roots and fly off with them, there are so many of them all over the bushes . . . Where's the bug gun?'

'Under the sink,' said Maj. Her mother opened the under-sink cupboard, hunting out the spray bottle of organic soap insecticide, the only form of chemical warfare she allowed in her garden.

'Mom, you should really get something more effective,' Maj said, as her mother went out. 'Something systemic, so the bugs'll bite the bushes and die of it.'

'Technofreak,' her mother said with good-natured scorn, as the screen door banged closed behind her.

'Oh, yeah,' Maj said, amused.

She glanced up at the kitchen clock. *Three o'clock already?* It was only three hours to the battle. The thought brought chills. The hair stood up all over her. *Food,* she thought, *and a fast review of our last maneuvers . . .*

She was too jumpy, already, for a big meal. Maj rummaged around in the fridge for a bowl of microwave noodles, made herself some more tea, and settled at the table to slip back into her workspace.

About a second later, it seemed, her bowl was empty, her tea was cold, and Laurent was looking at her from across the table, standing there in the middle of the kitchen and looking slightly bemused. 'Maj?' he said. 'I am sorry, you are virtual?'

'Huh? Not so it matters,' she said, surprised, for it had genuinely taken several moments for her to register him standing there. *I'm as preoccupied as he was this morning,* she thought. She glanced up at the clock. It was five-thirty. 'Hey, your stuff's there on the counter.' Maj looked at him carefully. 'Are you okay?'

'I feel fine,' Laurent said. And indeed he looked fine, better than anyone had a right to who had just been through the day and a half he'd had. 'This is it?'

'That package, yeah. Let me know if something doesn't fit. The invoice says they have a pickup van in the area if we need to return anything . . . all we need to do is call. Meantime, what do you want to eat? We should have something before we go to the battle . . . you'll be surprised how this kind of fighting takes it out of you.'

'Oh.' He stood there in his 'schoolboy' clothes and looked bemused. 'Maybe a sandwich?'

'Every kind of cold cut on earth is in the fridge,' Maj said, getting up to put her tea in the microwave. 'My brother is kind of a carnivore.' She grinned. 'We really have to introduce you to him, if you're ever awake at the same time. His hours have been a little weird lately . . . he has some kind of curling championship coming up.'

' "Curling"?'

'It's too weird to explain with mere words. It involves shoving a hunk of rock around on a sheet of ice with brooms and a handle. I'll show you later,' she said. 'Go on, get changed.'

He disappeared down the hall. When he came back, Maj had decided that a sandwich wasn't a bad idea, and was rooting around in the 'cool' cupboard for a loaf of rye. She glanced up. 'Hey,' she said, 'that looks good on you.'

He grinned that extremely charming smile that seemed to light up his whole face, partly by contrast. Laurent looked very sober most of the time, which, under the circumstances, Maj thought, was probably understandable. *When he gets old enough,* she thought, *he's going to need a stick to beat the girls off with, if he keeps that smile . . .*

'So, here,' Maj said. 'Baloney, mortadella, regular ham, Mom's favorite smoked Virginia ham which she will threaten out lives for eating, my father's head cheese, white bread, pumpernickel, rye, mayo . . .'

'Mustard?' Laurent said.

'In the fridge.'

He went to get it. 'It did not comment,' Laurent said, returning with it.

Maj smiled. 'It'll find something to say eventually. I

should warn you, don't leave its door open, or it'll call you "Adrienne".'

'Oh?'

'The Muffin likes to stand there and look in, pondering the mysteries of the universe.'

'Oh.' He started slathering mustard on some of the pumpernickel. 'But her proper name is Adrienne . . .'

'She won't answer to it. She decided some while back that Muffin is her name, and she won't answer to Adrienne any more.' Maj shrugged. 'We'll see if it lasts. She may change her mind in a few years when the other kids at school start ragging her about it.' She got a plate for her sandwich, then said, 'Speaking of names . . . we'll keep using Niko, huh? Just so she doesn't get confused. But I know the story behind the cover story.'

He nodded, that somber expression in place again. 'I am sorry,' Laurent said, 'not to really be related to you.'

The pain in his voice, though he was trying hard to cover it over, was considerable. Maj shook her head. 'While you're here,' she said, 'you are. So forget about it. But what do I call you in private? Laurent seems awfully formal.'

'Lari is the short form, the – nickname?'

'Oh. Larry?'

'Close,' he said. 'Larry,' he said, a little slowly, as if it were a word in a foreign language – but then again it was.

'It's just a short form of Lawrence. Your name, but the English version.'

'Okay. Larry.'

'Great,' Maj said. 'Now at least I won't have to shout at you and get no answer.'

Laurent grinned. 'It must have seemed silly. But it is hard to remember you have a new name.' Then the grin fell off, as if he was remembering something that made him uncomfortable. 'Larry is better.'

'Well, you'll still have to remember around the Muffin.'

'I think I will manage. Is there another plate?' She handed him one, and he put his sandwich on it and cut it in half. 'She will keep reminding me, I think . . .'

They went to sit down, and Maj rooted around in the fridge for her mother's perpetual jug of iced tea and brought it to the table. For a while they sat and ate comfortably enough, not saying anything; but Maj suddenly became aware that Laurent was looking at her, and she raised her eyebrows.

'You look worried,' he said.

She opened her mouth to protest that she didn't know what he was talking about . . . then laughed. 'The battle,' Maj said. 'I always get twitchy before these . . .'

'But it is virtual,' Laurent said, looking somewhat bemused.

'Well,' she said, 'there's virtual, and then there's virtual. Look—' She pushed the plate away and got up. 'We'll be a little early, but there's no harm in being the first ones into the hangar. Though wait half a second—'

She put her head out the back door and looked for her mother. She was crouched down behind some rosebushes, slaughtering aphids. 'Mom,' she said, 'my battle's in a little while. I want to take L-Niko along, but I don't want to sit at the table—'

'You use my machine, honey,' her mother said. 'Niko can use the chair in the den. I don't think Rick's going to be back until well after you're done.'

She let the door close. 'My brother usually uses the den link,' Maj said. 'Fortunately he's out of the picture at the moment. Come on, finish that up and we'll get you settled.'

A few minutes later they were both installed in separate rooms. Minutes after that, they were in Maj's workspace. Laurent looked around appreciatively again. 'Mine is nothing so nice,' he said. 'But maybe now it is over here, I can make some changes.'

'You had your space cloned over here?'

'My father took care of it last week,' he said. Laurent glanced around him. 'But it is very empty compared to this. All these books in the shelves . . . these are real works somewhere else?'

'Reference stuff mostly. Encyclopedias, almanacs, links to the news services. I'll show you how it's done after I get back from school tomorrow. Meanwhile—'

She paused by the version of her desk that lived in the workspace, and put her hand down on it. 'Computer . . .'

'Wide awake, boss.'

'Open access to *Cluster Rangers*. I need a guest authorization.'

There was a pause. 'Addition to account authorized,' said the computer. 'Is the authorization intended for the party presently in your workspace?'

'Yes.'

'Noted. Time limitations now apply to guest accounts. Fifty hours maximum.'

Maj rolled her eyes. This was more than enough time to get anyone she could think of addicted to the game . . . which was doubtless the designers' intention. 'Thank you,' she said. 'Ready?'

'Ready now. Preferred area of ingress?'

' "Hangar 1." '

'Hangar 1 access ready.'

She went over to the door in the wall, opened it. 'Come on in.'

Laurent followed her in. On the other side of the door was a huge empty space with a shiny concrete floor. The walls were a long way off, and were also painted concrete with large tool closets and metal equipment shelving pushed up against them. From the corrugated metal ceiling hung lights so bright they almost hurt to look at, and in the middle of it all sat Maj's Arbalest fighter.

It was a long, sharp-nosed black shape somewhat reminiscent of the old SR-71 Blackbird, but stubbier, and not so 'flattened' in cross-section, and it was shiny mirror-black, not matte, for protection against the light-weapons. The wings were swept back much more acutely, and the wing-roots were much broader, partly to support the weight of the 'Crossbow' pumped laser cannons that hung under them on each side.

'This is yours?' Laurent breathed.

'Yup,' Maj said, as they walked toward it. 'Well, my group's, anyway. The basic design, I mean. We've all made modifications to the design, here and there. But it's not too bad.' She paused and just took a moment to admire it.

Laurent was walking around it with his mouth very satisfyingly open. Maj was pleased. Whatever else might be going on inside this new visitor, he plainly had taste.

'Suit,' she said to the air. Her spacesuit appeared on her – again one of the game's standard suits, but customized with the Group of Seven's black eight-ball patch (though the numeral was a seven instead) on the shoulders. It was similar to gee suits being used today by those pilots who insisted on flying their fighters 'genuinely' rather than virtually, but it had much more attention paid to the insulation. Even fighter pilots do not normally have to worry about being dumped out of their craft in deep space, or having to wait there for pickup for prolonged periods.

'Games controller,' Maj said.

'Yes, ma'am,' said the game's computer.

'Would you provide a suit for my guest, please?'

'Yes, ma'am. Will he be participating in flight?'

'Flight, yes. Not fighting, though.'

'Control sequencing unchanged, then.'

'That's right.'

'Next order.'

'On hold.'

'Yes, ma'am.'

A sudden squeak came from Laurent as he was heading around from the other side of the fighter. 'Suit too tight?' Maj said.

'Uh, no, it just surprised me.'

She restrained herself from shaking her head and commenting on how much his home system plainly left to be desired. Costuming – changing body covering or, for that matter, body shape – was one of the most basic virtual utilities. If they won't even let people dress up the way they want to—! 'Well, no more serious surprises,' she said. 'Come on, let's get up into the cockpit. We've got a short jump to make before we take the long one.'

He hurried along beside her. 'Where is this? I mean, where are we supposed to be?'

'It's a hangar facility on Amrit, the third moon of the gas giant Dolorosa,' Maj said. 'I don't know how much that helps you. Come on, get in. The aft ladder is on the other side – walk underneath.'

She clambered up into the cockpit. 'Let me know if that seat suits you,' she said. 'The program should have fixed it.'

There was some clunking and bumping as Laurent wriggled himself into the number-two seat behind her. 'It's – snug,' he said.

'Partly for protection against those high-G turns,' she said. 'You'll be glad of it later. Helmet,' she said.

Maj's helmet appeared, a perfectly transparent dome that faired into her suit apparently seamlessly. It was solid plex. Maj knew other players who trusted the new force-field helmets, but herself, she preferred something that didn't need a power source, no matter how 'guaranteed' the power sources were.

'But this is, well, virtual,' Laurent said, sounding a little dubious. 'Do we really need these?'

Maj laughed. 'You breathe a little vacuum, and you'll find out whether you need it or not.'

'But we couldn't really suffocate, or—'

'Yes, I know, it's a game, but isn't it more fun to play a game and pretend it's *not* a game?' Maj said. 'You ready? We should get going. Got yourself strapped in?'

It was the usual five-point harness, and as usual took a little doing for him to get all fastened in the first time. When Laurent was helmeted and secure, Maj said, 'Hangar control . . .'

'Working,' said a drier, tinnier voice than the game controller's.

'Evacuate the hangar.'

She powered up the Arbalest's Morgenroth drivers while the air hissed out of the place. 'I should warn you,' Maj said. 'The game designer has built high-G resistance into the human stress parameters. Some of the things we may do later can look pretty scary. And don't freak out if you see me doing something that can normally break a ship like this in two. It won't. It'll just *look* like it will.'

'Oh, well, then, I am reassured,' Laurent said. Maj was tempted to burst out laughing at his tone of voice, which suggested that reassurance was thinner on the ground in his mental environment than he would have liked.

'Hangar evacuated,' said the hangar control voice.

'Okay,' Maj said. 'Here we go.'

She cut in the vectored locals and pushed the Arbalest up. The scream of the engines was perfectly audible. Looking in the mirrored canopy above her, Maj could see Laurent's eyebrows go up, but he made no comment. 'Crack the ceiling,' she told the hangar.

The center sections of the ceiling started to roll away from the centerline, with a last hiss as a little pressure equalization happened. Outside was not a perfect vacuum by any means. Amrit was a large enough moon to have kept some of the heavier gases, and as Maj eased in the locals they bobbed up into a cloud of them, above which some light source was dimly visible, like the moon above cloud.

'You wouldn't like it out there,' Maj said to Laurent. 'There's a lot of swept-up methane in the atmosphere. Amrit is a "shepherd moon". Another good reason for a helmet, if something should go wrong with the ship. The stuff gets full of organic compounds after a while . . . and the *stink!* You wouldn't want to know . . .'

'I can do without stink,' Laurent said, looking up and around with interest.

'Good. Here we go . . .'

She took the Arbalest straight up into the cloudy silvery dimness. Toward the zenith, that silveriness started to get stronger. 'The moon?' Laurent said.

'Not quite . . .'

They burst up out of the cloud. Twelve degrees down from the zenith hung the source of the light. Laurent took a long, sudden breath, and did not let it out.

Hanging there above the curve of Amrit's atmosphere

was the Cluster, in unimpeded view . . . and it was a view worth seeing. NGC 2057 was one of the so-called 'Guardian Angel' globular star clusters soaring above and below the plane of the Milky Way galaxy – a gigantic spherical array of stars, radiating out like an explosion of multicolored jewels from a core where the stars were clustered together almost too tightly to make them out as separate entities. Many of them, too, were short-period variables, so that they visibly swelled and shrank as you looked at them, like live things breathing, burning sedately in blinding fire.

'This is the Seraphim Cluster,' Maj said. 'A long time ago a very old, very wise species lived here – the Danir. They had science beyond anything we know . . . and they fought terrible wars with another species also native to the Cluster, an evil species that we know little about. They're all gone, now. But an explorer found the Daniri science, and the living machines that were maintaining it, on the Heartworld of the cluster. The machines told the explorer to find others like him, the outcasts, the curious, the people who couldn't leave well enough alone . . . the people who believed in standing up for the defenseless and trying to stop the bad things that happened all around them. They would be equipped with weapons that would make them invincible . . . if they used them properly. They would descend from the Cluster into the Galaxy with their new weapons and become the defenders of the right, facing down crime and evil wherever they found it. They would be hunted down by both the evildoers and by those who didn't understand their mission . . . but if they persevered, they would triumph. They would become the Cluster Rangers.' She grinned at him. 'Or, *we* would. Some of us.'

'You mean, you pretend to be—'

Maj laughed softly, glanced up in the cockpit mirror. 'While you're in it, "pretending" doesn't describe it at all,' she said. 'Your part of the Net isn't very virtual, is it?'

Laurent's look was wry. 'I think,' he said, 'the government doesn't like the idea of people escaping from reality.'

Maj thought briefly of an ancient recorded interview she had seen with a writer who lived in the middle of the last century. *What kind of people do you think are most concerned about other people escaping from reality?* he had said. *The jailers . . .* She made a face.

'Typical. But look.'

They had been making steady progress up and away from the cloudtops of Amrit as Maj talked. Now they were making for the terminator; and the light of Dolorosa's primary, red-golden Hekse, started to grow behind the edges of the atmosphere, lines of blue-dominated spectrum growing brighter all the time. Maj smiled slightly, and kicked the drivers in, making for the light at increased speed. All around them, a faint soft shrilling was audible, almost musical, like tiny bells being rung at a great distance – a shivering, shining sound. But then they came over the edge, over the terminator, up into the light . . .

. . .and space was full of the sound. The system's primary hung there, blazing, shining on the ship and on Amrit and on the huge peach-and-brick-banded curvature of Dolorosa, hanging at one o'clock; and the sound of the sun smote them full on, a profound boom, like a gong but sounding many notes at once, all shivering, like the echo of the stars far away. It was of course the same sound, only made bearable here by immense distance – starsong, the game designer's idea of the music of the spheres. Beyond the sun, and producing not that huge boom, but rather a much more tenuous, silvery sound, lay the galaxy. Much of it was obscured by interstellar dust, from this 'height.' But the nearest arm, lying right across a third of the visible sky, shone fierce and clear – not the delicate light you got from the rest of the Milky Way as seen from Earth on a clear night, but bright, definite, and immense. Best of all, though, you could hear its stars shining, a multifarious and splendid harmony across the terrible distance, and all around, silent, you could feel empty space listening.

'It is beautiful,' Laurent said very softly behind Maj.

'You got that in one,' Maj said. It was the sound, though, that had done it for her the first time – the game designer's idea that, if you could hear explosions in space, well, what was the shining of a star but a very large, controlled, prolonged explosion? It had given her the shivers then, and it did so now. But there was no time to waste. The others would be meeting on the bigger moon, Jorkas, in a matter of minutes.

'I wish my father could see this . . .' Laurent said, very quietly.

'He will,' Maj said. 'I'll make sure of it.' It was all she could find to say immediately that wouldn't sound soppy or artificial. That image of a man, alone, in a little harshly lighted room with no windows, while someone with a gun and a nasty expression stood over him, had recurred to her a few times since she'd spoken to her father. It was probably born of seeing too many old movies. But Maj knew that, though the details of that kind of intimidation might have changed over the years, the mindset had not. There were still plenty of people who didn't mind hurting other people to get what they wanted. The thought of Laurent's *father* being stuck in such a situation . . . or worse, her own . . . It made her shudder.

'Could I – is there any chance I could fly this?' Laurent said, in a very small voice.

Maj grinned at that, understanding the instant attraction. 'Not tonight, Laurent. We've got business to take care of. For tonight, just sit still and enjoy the ride. But I have a sim built into my workspace to practice on. Tomorrow you can fly all day, if you want, and get the feel of it. Who knows? We might need a new pilot one of these days, and I can't see why the squadron would refuse a talented one . . .'

She kicked in the Morgenroths at full, and made her way around the other side of Dolorosa. Just the far side of the gas giant's terminator Maj found Jorkas sailing along toward them, seeming leisurely as always in this system where its less massive brothers and sisters mostly tore around their primary as if their tails were on fire. Maj made for the pole, where even at this distance she could see the big streetlight circle-and-7 that marked the Group's base.

Five minutes later they were settling into the 'parking bay,' a circular force-fielded area that was otherwise open to space and the spectacular views of Dolorosa and the Cluster. Eight other Arbalests were there, the syncrete under them glowing softly in token that their engines were alive and on standby; and their pilots stood in a small cluster, talking, occasionally waving an arm or two. A large spherical hologram hovered glowing over the 'crete to one side, mostly being ignored. One of the pilots was pacing back and forth, back and forth, with metronomic regularity.

'Shih Chin,' Maj said, as she popped the canopy. 'She always does that. She gets tense.'

'Will they mind that I'm here?' Laurent said.

Maj opened her mouth to say 'no,' and then started to say 'yes,' and then said, 'I don't care if they do. But I doubt they will, once they understand you're just along for the ride. Just be friendly, and leave them to me.'

They walked across the syncrete toward the others. Heads turned as they came, and Kelly said, 'Maj, who's your copilot?'

'God,' Maj said, laughing, 'if anybody. This is a passenger . . . he's a cousin of mine, just in from Hungary. Niko, this is the Group of Seven.'

He did not make the response a lot of them would have expected, which Maj suspected pleased them. The name 'Group of Seven' was as much of a joke about its members' wildly conflicting schedules as about anything else. If you could get as many as seven of them together in one place, it was an event, even when there were eleven of them total. Niko, though, just smiled at them. 'Hello,' he said.

'This is Kelly,' Maj said, indicating the tall freckly redhead. 'Shih Chin—' She stopped pacing just long enough to smile. 'Sander—' Dark-haired Sander waved. 'Chel, and Mairead—' Mairead shook her blazing red curls out of her eyes, grinned a little at Laurent. Chel, looking taller and broader than usual in the spacesuit, waved. 'Bob—' He nodded to Laurent with a preoccupied look.

'And Robin and Del.'

'Hi,' Robin said, and Del bowed a little, idiosyncratically formal as always. Maj waggled her eyebrows at them, grinned, but didn't say anything else, for she saw them a little more frequently than the others in the Group . . . since Robin and Del were also Net Force Explorers. Big, blocky Del was attached to the New York area, where his dad and mom both worked at a large law firm, and little slender Robin with her retropunk blue Mohawk was somewhere in one of the LA suburbs, living with a dad who worked for Rocketdyne. They had never met physically, but then lots of the Net Force Explorers hadn't, their online meetings, by and large, being considered to be real enough to get by with. In any case, their status with net Force wasn't something that they went into a lot with the other members of the Group of Seven. Partly this was because having made it into the Net Force Explorers when so many people wanted to get in, was something of a plum . . . and partly because it struck them all that bragging about it was not only unnecessary, but possibly unwise. Occasionally Net Force Explorers found themselves working together on projects which were not precisely public knowledge, and which were probably better staying that way. They preferred to keep the profile of that part of their involvement with the Explorers low. However, there was no rule that said they couldn't have fun together 'off duty' – if there was any such thing for three young people so thoroughly committed to the jobs they intended to have some day, and if there was any justice.

'Glad you could make it,' Bob said. 'We've been going over strat-tac again . . .'

'And we are *completely screwed*,' Shih Chin muttered.

'We are not,' said Kelly, 'will you *stop over-reacting!*'

There was a brief silence. 'Nerves,' said Kelly, with some embarrassment.

'Yeah. Look, forget it.'

A mutter of agreement went round the group. 'How long now?' Mairead said.

'Ten minutes to the positions filed with the master tactics computer.'

'Oh, I hate this part,' Del muttered. 'Once we get up there and start shooting things, everything will be fine.'

'Assuming we last that long,' Kelly said.

'Hungarian, huh?' said Chel. 'Well, Goulash, you're in for a real show today . . . assuming we survive the first ten minutes.'

Maj opened her mouth to say something cutting to Chel, but Laurent grinned and said, 'Goulash? I like goulash. And if you make it right, with the really hot paprika, it's got a bite.' He bounced a little in the light gravity, still smiling. 'Separates the men from the boys.'

'Paprika?' said Bob. 'That's right, it's a kind of chilli, isn't it? My dad grows chillis, and he—'

'You can talk about your male macho chilli-eating stuff later, for pity's sake,' Maj said. 'Niko, better have a look at the diagram, you'll see what's cooking . . .'

They went over to it, the others following by ones and twos. The hologram was mostly filled with the planet Didion, where the Arbalests would be fighting down and dirty in the atmosphere with many, many others.

'It's a "built" planet,' Maj said, as Laurent walked around the hologram, peering at it. 'It may look green . . . but everything about Didion is artificial. It's constructed, from the core out . . . there are thousands of levels. It was the library for all this part of space once, until the Archon moved in and took things over. Now it's been reamed out and stuffed full of weapons, killerbots, crawling code . . . you name it. Nasty place, and the nerve center for all the Archon's operations in this part of space. But there's a way down inside, and if we can once fight our way down to the surface and get in there—'

'And there, of course, is the problem,' Bob said. The surface of the planet on the hologram disappeared to reveal the way into the core – a complex and twisting path of conduits and tunnels.

'It's a body, with a brain,' Maj said. 'What it needs . . . is a lobotomy.'

'Icepicks R Us,' said Bob. The others groaned.

'Bob,' Shih Chin said with good-natured disgust, 'you are so *retro* sometimes.'

'A lot of other groups are going to be trying to beat us to it,' Mairead said. 'We intend to be first . . . or at least real close behind first.'

'First or nothing,' Chel said. 'Death or glory.'

Laurent stood looking thoughtfully at the diagram – the globe, the involved way in to the heart of it, the 'sensitive area' hidden at the heart. 'This looks,' he said, 'kind of familiar.'

There was a subdued chuckle from some of the others. 'Yeah,' Shih Chin said. 'It's a reworking of an old archetype. There have been some additions to it, though. Take a look—'

They spent the next few minutes going over the worst of the boobytraps – as much to show them to Laurent as to remind themselves. 'The worst things are the shipeaters,' Del said, pointing at the two separate places where the 'eaters' were known to have been positioned in the main accesses. 'They're nothing small that you could shoot up. They're jaws that come out of the walls – they *are* the walls, actually – and munch you up. Nasty.'

'If you just get shot up and die, you can at least reclaim the points inherent in your shipbuild in another round of the game,' Maj said to Laurent. 'But if something completely destroys your ship and you can't recover the material for salvage, you have to start over from scratch . . . buy your way back into the construction program and then sometimes wait a month or two before the resources are available to build your new ship . . .'

'Like real life,' Laurent said.

'All too much like it,' Kelly said.

From the direction of the buildings in their base complex, a klaxon began to sound. 'That's it, troops,' Shih Chin said, and with a look of great relief headed off toward her ship.

'*Chinnn!!*' Bob and Del and Mairead shouted after her.

'Oh . . . I forgot.' She came back to the rest of them.

'Ready?' Bob said, putting out a hand.

Shih Chin put her hand on top of Bob's, and then one after another, the Group piled hands up on top of one another. 'Oh, come on, Goulash,' Bob said to Laurent then, and shyly, Laurent put his hand on top of all of theirs.

'Seven for seven,' Bob said. 'Or nine, or ten. However many we are. Yeah?'

'*Yeah!*' they all shouted.

'Now let's go kick the Archon's big green butt,' Shih Chin said, 'and be back home in time for popcorn and a late movie.'

Everyone headed hurriedly for their fighters. Shortly Maj and Laurent were back in their seats, and all around them the scream of Morgenroths coming up to speed was becoming deafening. 'This planet,' Laurent said, nearly shouting over the noise, 'it is in this system?'

'Nope,' Maj said. 'Fourteen light-years away.'

Laurent's eyes widened as the nine ships lifted up and away from the surface of Jorkas together, in formation. 'And we are going to get there in ten minutes?'

'In about a second and a half, actually,' Maj said, checking the readouts for the sizeable part of the Arbalest's

110

computer which managed the squeezefield synchronization. 'If we had a jumpgate, it would be even faster. But that
uses a lot of power, and the gate structure is vulnerable at
either end to sabotage. However, we have enough ships to
do it the other way.' She glanced around. The others were
slowing down, preparing.

'What way?'

'Hang on,' she said, and meant it. The first time, it was
always a surprise . . .

'Ready, Seven?' Bob's voice came down the ship's
comm.

'Ready!' Maj said. Seven other voices said, '*Ready!*'

'Synch starts – *now!*'

The squeezefield sequence cut in. Maj watched the
guidance laser jump from craft to craft, knitting them
together in a many-times reflected webwork of light. The
hypermass augmentation sequence started—

And then the stars streaked in to collapse around them,
molded themselves flaming to the shapes of the ships,
pushed the ships and their pilots unbearably *inward* on
themselves in a wave of spatially-compressed light and a
deafening scream of sound—

Everything vanished. And then the stars blazed out
again, leaping back out to their proper positions, and
leaving the formation of Arbalests falling toward the
surface of the planet Didion . . .

Laurent was gasping. 'You – you—!'

'You can either poke holes in the universe to get where
you're going,' Maj said, 'which some people suspect is bad
for its structure . . . or you can wrap it around you like a
coat, go where you're going, and then take the coat off
again. It's all the same coat. Everything in it touches
everything else . . .'

That was as much theory as Maj intended to get into at the moment, for there was a lot to do, a lot of instruments to check and double check in the next minute or so. The cockpit was filling up with nervous background chatter from the others as they did what Maj was doing – made sure the weapons were hot and loose, the Morgenroths answering properly. Below them, streaks of fire and puffs of smoke and long streamers of contrail in the upper and middle atmosphere told them that the Battle of Didion was already in progress, and heating up.

'*Ready?*' Bob said from his Arbalest, taking the squad leadership and point this time out. He had devised the strategy they would be using on the way in, and therefore he got to die first if anything went wrong.

'All set, big B,' Maj said.

'*Ready, Bob.*'

'*Let's do it, already!*'

'*Seven for seven,*' Bob said. '*Go. Go. Go.*'

Nine Arbalest fighters fell at ever-increasing speed toward the surface of Didion. From the back seat of one of them came a yell of pure and not entirely inappropriate joy, and in the front seat, the pilot smiled, settled one arm deep into the field that handled the firing controls, and got ready to show her houseguest a good time.

Six thousand miles away, the Major was sitting in business class on a domestic flight to Vienna, from which she would have to catch yet another flight to Zurich, the nearest spaceplane port. She much disliked having to pass through Switzerland, but at the moment it was unavoidable. Speed was of the essence, and she had other things than the wretched Swiss on her mind.

'He has not left the house, Major,' said the voice down

the hushed and scrambled Net link she was using from the booth at the back of business class.

'Good. A small blessing, if nothing else. What are his hosts doing?'

'Having a quiet day at home, it would seem. The mother has been working in the garden. The father has been in the household Net mostly, not out in the public nets at all. The daughter and the boy are in the Net as well.'

'In the boy's accounts?'

'No. Though they could be at any time. His father had his son's account information installed on a North American server.'

'Well, that should hardly be a problem for us. Break into the accounts. I want them completely searched.'

'Unfortunately,' said her contact, 'the server is not the one to which they were originally moved. The new server is one which is used by several US government agencies . . . and it is regrettably extremely well protected. We cannot get at it.'

She muttered something rude under her breath. 'Well, at the very least I want the boy watched and listened to wherever he goes in the public Nets. He's likely enough to drop some useful information where it can be heard.'

'But, Major, except for the Greens' household Net, he has been nowhere except in a proprietary system – and that as a guest on the professor's daughter's account. And the proprietary systems routinely have top-flight filters which keep outside access limited to registered subscribers—'

'Well, *subscribe!*'

'We did. But it takes twenty-four hours to approve the credit. And besides, our country's domains are blocked. We had to go in through a Transylvanian domain address, and for that we had to get the usual clearances—'

Bureaucracy, she thought in anguish, and covered her face with one hand. It had its uses, but most of them rarely did her any good.

'Just do it,' the Major said. 'Once inside the proprietary system, you should find a fair amount of information about the girl – her habits, how often she uses the system, and so on. I want a complete report on that. Meanwhile, how is the search for the father doing?'

'There is good news there, Major. The techs working on one of his research associates have produced some results. They said he had gone north for holidays several times in the last year, even though as far as they know, he had no family or friends up there. His excuse was that he had been fishing.'

'I daresay he had . . . though I think it more likely that the kind of fish we have in the lakes up there were not what he had in mind.'

'Perhaps not. He made some mention of the places he had gone. We are questioning people in those towns now . . . and one woman there says she thinks she saw him two days ago.'

The Major smiled. 'The increased surveillance at the borders may yet pay off. Increase the searches in the north, then . . . Also, find out if any of our own people know anything about fishing.'

There was a silence at the other end. 'Excuse me, Major?'

'You heard me. I want them kitted out with appropriate equipment and sent up north. Darenko may actually have *been* fishing. In fact, he may be doing it now. A capable fisherman can live for a good while in the countryside without needing to set foot in a town where anyone can see him . . .'

'Uh, yes, Major, I'll take care of it.'

'Do so first thing in the morning. Then get into the Net and see what the boy is doing. I will have to be ready to move shortly when I get there . . . and I want as much information on hand as possible to guide me.'

'Yes, Major.'

'Now, what about the professor? You had leads you were still researching.'

The response sounded somewhat nervous. 'He has ties to Net Force.'

Her breath hissed out. 'We knew about that. His daughter is in the Net Force Explorers, after all.'

'No, Major. Closer ties than that.'

'I see. Can you be more specific?'

'I'm sorry.'

'Very well. I will contact you before I leave Zurich.'

She closed the connection down, took a moment to compose herself, and headed out into the cabin again. *Twelve hours or so,* she thought, *and I will be there. And after that . . . we will go about the business of taking back what is rightfully ours.*

The Major settled herself in her comfortable seat again, smoothing down the handsome businesswoman's skirt suit which was her 'uniform' for this particular mission. *Poor Laurent,* she thought. *Enjoy yourself while you can. There will be little enough enjoyment for you when we get you home . . .*

Five

Maj woke surprisingly early. It was what her mother referred to as 'happy wake-up,' the kind that happens when you've successfully finished a job and your whole system knows it. You wake up completely rested and feeling ready for anything, though the hour is patently absurd. On this particular morning, dawn was just turning things pink and gold at the edges in the eastern sky when Maj wandered out to the kitchen, enjoying the blessed stillness before the rest of the family really got moving.

Classes felt like they were half a day away, though in reality she would have to be ready to leave in an hour and a half. She put the kettle on, then slipped into her workspace, leaving it 'open' to the kitchen so that she could see if Laurent or the Muffin surfaced all of a sudden.

E-mail immediately appeared all over the desk, which – in this overlapped merging of reality and virtual reality – was stuck to the kitchen table. A quick reconnoiter of the contents revealed many congratulatory notes from the other members of the Group. The Group of Seven had done spectacularly last night. Part of it, truth be told, was just Bob's good planning. He had a twisty mind, that one, and made a good squadron leader in a fighter-group situation.

But the rest of it was so much a matter of teamwork that Maj hardly knew where to start praising the others – Shih Chin's go-for-broke courage, Kelly's chilly accuracy with the pumped lasers, Mairead's eyes-in-the-back-of-her-head that missed nothing happening around her, whether to friend or foe. They had done well from the standpoint of scoring. All of them got in, shot up a goodly portion of Didion's insides, and they all got out again before the cluster nuke went off inside the station.

There had been disappointments. They had not been involved in the final attack that fought its way in to emplace the nuke. They had not made it as far into Didion's tortuous insides as Maj had hoped they would. Weapons charges ran low, and the Group of Seven had had to beat it out of there before the Black Arrows caught up with them and minced them all. Still, the retreat had been orderly, and they had been on hand for the Big Bang, and had been included in the distribution of bonus points for those involved in the planet's destruction. The Archon would think twice about trying to establish a base so close to the Cluster Rangers' home space again. And now the Rangers could get back to concentrating on carrying the battle deeper into the Archon's space, working slowly on the master plan to force him out of the galaxy entirely . . .

Maj smiled. *Entirely satisfactory,* she thought. *The whole thing.* And she had gotten an odd charge out of having someone in the seat behind her for a change, someone absolutely blown out of the water by everything that was happening. Oh, eventually little Laurent would get over the novelty of it all, and calm down. But in the meantime, his unbridled enthusiasm was too cute for words.

Maj finished sorting through her mail, making sure she told everyone what she thought of them – an unusually pleasant task since, today, she thought everyone in the Group was wonderful. Once that was done, she sat quietly with her tea for a few minutes, basking in the glow of the previous evening's success.

It was not an unbroken glow, though. The sound of a somewhat lost-sounding little voice saying, *I wish my father could see this* . . . was still very much with her.

'Computer . . .' Maj said.

'Ready, boss.'

'Put me together a general review of recent history of the Calmani Republic. Video, audio, and supplementary text.'

'Depth?'

'Average.'

It took the system a few seconds to assemble what she wanted from her workspace's link to the Britannica databases. 'Ready.'

'Go . . .'

The pictures began to display themselves all around her, a little grainy at first, as the oldest flatfilm and holos tended to be when rechanneled for virtuality – soldiers marching down country roads, politicians making angry speeches, great crowds gathered together in city streets. Calmani was only one of the remnants of numerous countries that had torn themselves apart just before or after the turn of the millennium, due to the exacerbation of old hatreds or new tensions. Sometimes the troubles were caused by newly independent peoples using their sudden freedom to resurrect the arguments of two or three or five centuries past, old 'grudge matches' interrupted by the interference of one or another of the great powers and resumed at the first possible moment. Or sometimes the rivalries that broke out involved one side or the other of the old border suddenly having more money or more power than their neighbours did. While everyone had been poor together, things had been fine – but when one country suddenly started doing better than the others around it, tensions rose. For these and many other kinds of reasons, some of the local histories in that part of the world had turned unimaginably bloody.

Maj watched the images of soldiers and speechmakers unfolding around her and thought, suddenly, of the last time she and her mom had gone crabbing together. After you caught the crabs, you hauled them out of the trap and put them in a bucket before taking them home. Naturally the crabs all started trying to escape – but their preferred method for doing this seemed to involve pulling each other down in order to climb up the others' bodies and get on top. None of the crabs seemed to notice that, as a result of all the pulling down, none of them were escaping. Now Maj thought of all those small countries, desperate, struggling, and yet only succeeding in keeping one another down.

Elsewhere, though, power had changed hands with relatively little fuss beyond mass demonstrations in the streets and some shootings of people in high places. Romania was one of these places. After many years of truly astonishing repression under a Marxist-style dictator, the country shook him off suddenly and relatively unbloodily, and settled down into what everyone had thought would be a slow but steady process of 'Westernization.' But there were still surprises in store. After the Balkan difficulties of the turn of the millennium had trailed off and a long weary quiet had settled over the area, suddenly the nationalist urge awakened in Romania, and over the space of several months the country shuddered, convulsed, and split itself in three. The southernmost and most urban part, which named itself Oltenia after its northern hills, kept the cities of Bucharest and Constante (and incidentally most of the region's trade with the West, since it had the Black Sea ports at Constant and Mangalia). The midpost part of the country became Transylvania as a nation as well as a region. It had stayed fairly calm and settled, even while the dust of secession was still in the air, and had continued to do a brisk business in tourism to the former haunts of Vlad Dracula, both for those tourists interested in the ancient Voivod as a nationalist hero who fought off the Huns, and those more interested in his (theoretical) career as a vampire.

The northernmost area of what the news people routinely called 'the-former-Romania,' the area which now called itself the Calmani Republic and contained most of the mountain chain stretching down from that area, had at first seemed likely to go the same way as Oltenia. But when the revolution had almost finished, and the candidates whom it seemed the local people wanted to run things were about to take power, there came a hiccup that took everyone by surprise. Several of the candidates for the new ten-man Senate died under strange and violent circumstances – shot in the streets by unknown assailants, or bombed in their beds – and other candidates pulled out of the Senate within days. When this new and terrible cloud of dust settled, there were only three Senators left, and the new small country as a whole was so unnerved that no one argued much when the three of them took power as a caretaker government until a new set of elections could be held, if they ever would be . . .

'I don't know,' she suddenly heard her father say, from down the hall. 'I'll ask, though. Maj?'

He put his head around the kitchen door. Her dad was wearing his sweats, which was normal this time of morning; usually he went out running as early as possible on summer workdays to take advantage of the cooler temperatures.

'Yeah, Dad?'

'Were you going to order some workout clothes for Niko? He's going to run with me. All he needs are sweats, nothing fancy. And he'll need shoes.'

'Sure, I'll take care of it. He'll have to tell me his shoe size, though . . . the machine's no good at that. At least none of our machines are . . . The GearOnline computer might be able to pull something from the measurements it took the other day. Just in case, what's the size?'

'Thirty-six,' Laurent said, putting his head around from behind Maj's father.

She goggled at him. 'What are you doing up at this awful hour?'

'It is lunchtime in Europe,' Laurent said.

'I don't mean that. I mean, not *just* that. It's not that long ago that we finished things up!' And indeed Maj was feeling a little grainy around the eyeballs herself from lack of sleep.

But Laurent grinned at her. 'I am fine.'

'I'm not so sure. Is thirty-six really a shoe size where you come from?'

'Yes.'

'Okay,' Maj said. 'I'll tell GearOnline . . . we'll see what they make of it.'

Her father and Laurent vanished around the door again, down the hall and out the front door into the morning. Maj raised her eyebrows, then said to the computer, 'Go ahead again . . .'

A few moments later she was watching things get strange in Calmani, twenty years or so ago. The 'troika' caretaker government took office and functioned well enough for a few months. But then two of them died, also under strange circumstances . . . and the country was kept so busy by trying to work out what the third one was going to do that they had little time or, later, opportunity, to find out exactly what had happened to the others. They were too busy dealing with their new ruler, Cluj.

Daimon Cluj was an elder statesman, a child of the bad old days when Ceaucescu was losing his grip on a country he had dominated ruthlessly with the connivance of the old Soviet Union. Some never forgave him, or the Soviet Union for that matter, for growing so weak that the 'good old days' of absolute order went away – the days when there was no drug problem and little crime in the streets because drug dealers and criminals were routinely tortured to death when they were caught. Days when there was no political unrest because anyone who got unrestful was arrested and shot.

Cluj, remembering those good old days, was determined to bring them back. And with the help of some thousands of vicious hired thugs – no one knew for sure where they came from, but there were plenty of such people still wandering covertly around the region, looking for some-one to hire them and turn them loose – he brought those old days back, in spades. He established an old-fashioned one-man dictatorship, Marxist-Leninist in spirit, full of talk about solidarity and brotherhood and the people, but in fact all about keeping Cluj himself in power, and putting his country 'back the way it should have been.' His version of 'should have been' involved large numbers of secret police, industry being taken over by the government and making what the government thought it could make, people eating what they were told to eat and seeing what entertainment or news they were told to watch, and otherwise keeping quiet and behaving themselves like enlightened citizens of an enlightened socialist state.

This all went well enough for several months, and people saw trains running on time and markets with food to sell – not a whole lot of different kinds of food, but a lot in terms of quantity – and drug dealers and thieves being put up against walls and shot. There was a lot of good feeling expressed about this. But then the prices of food in the markets began to rise, and the trains, though they ran on time, were not allowed to go any further than the Oltenian or Transylvanian or Hungarian border; and as for the New Army, the grim-faced men with the submachine guns, it seemed no one had given much thought as to what they would do when they ran out of drug dealers to shoot.

Predictably, they turned their attention elsewhere, closer to home, to the ordinary people they had 'liberated.' The secret police – no one called them that to their faces and Cluj's name for the organization was the Interior Security Forces – ran out of organized crime figures to terrorize, and started in on those who were neither organized nor criminals, like the people of Calmani's larger towns, Iasi and Galati and Suceava, who were assumed to be 'decadent' because they lived in cities. Those who had no reason to be 'living in luxury' were turned out of their homes and driven into the countryside to work on collective farms and be re-educated out of the decadent ways. But not everyone was driven out. Some, the ones that the Government – meaning Cluj – wanted something out of, were permitted to stay in the cities . . . but they had to work for the privilege.

Laurent's father, Maj now realized, was one of these. A scientist would be useful . . . a biologist much more so.

And so very specialized and talented a biologist would be a big asset. *They would never willingly let him go,* Maj thought. Especially when things were beginning to heat up a little over there, as they were at the moment. Oltenia and Transylvania were doing well for themselves – despite Cluj denouncing them every other day as malicious or deluded lackeys of the Imperialist West. They were building (or in some cases rebuilding) infrastructures to support an increasingly more affluent population. They had access to the Net, and much better access than the poor censored (and bugged) public-service terminals which were all Cluj would permit for the people other than his military and creative elite.

Oltenia and Transylvania were actually making noises about joining the European Union. And worse, on the northern border of Cluj's country, the Moldovan Republic had just concluded an arms deal with Ukraine. Cluj had apparently found this particular piece of news unnerving, and Maj thought she knew why. Though his ground forces were vicious and had plenty of small arms, Cluj was short on tanks and had no long-range weaponry worth speaking of. To his mind, a deal between Ukraine and Moldova could only mean one thing— Moldavia was planning to invade while he was vulnerable. This was obvious to Cluj because it was what he would have done himself.

At a time like this, Maj thought grimly, *there's only one thing Cluj's mind is going to be on. Weapons. He needs weapons.*

And Dad said that the Calmani government was beginning to look at Laurent's dad's work as something besides medical technology . . .

Maj shivered. 'That's enough,' she said to the computer. 'Virtual call. Tag it non-urgent/accept if convenient. Leave as a message if unavailable or no response.'

'Whom are you calling, boss?'

'James Winters.'

'Working.'

There was a pause.

A moment later, 'Maj,' James Winters said. 'Good morning.' He was at his desk in his office at Net Force – a plain office, with some steel bookcases and a laminated desk, covered with work as always. The Venetian blinds were pulled up to show the mirror-coated windows – with one exception – revealing an inspiring view of the sunny parking lot.

'Mr Winters,' Maj said. 'Wow, you get up early.'

'Actually I slept in this morning,' he said, and grinned very slightly, so that it was hard for Maj to work out whether he was pulling her leg or not. 'But congratulations for taking so long to make this call. You're learning the art of restraint.'

Maj blushed. The last time they had worked closely together, Winters had upbraided her for being impatient. Maj didn't think she was particularly impatient – it wasn't her fault if she could figure things out faster than some people, and make up her mind *much* faster. Unfortunately she suspected James Winters of *perceiving* her as impatient . . . and perception was everything, in the game she was preparing to play in Net Force. Assuming they ever hired her . . . which would almost certainly be a decision that would have to pass across this man's desk.

'Restraint?' Maj said, playing the innocent for the moment.

'Must be at least a day since you found out what was going on,' he said. 'I would have thought you would have called to pump me yesterday.'

Maj could only smile at that, and at the idea that this man could be pumped without his permission. 'No,' she said, 'that's not what I'm interested in at the moment.'

'Oh? What, then?' He glanced at the one window that didn't show the parking lot. Maj knew that window was tasked to show the view in Winter's back yard at home, where a small brown bird was currently pecking enthusiastically on an empty bird-feeder.

'I didn't know you had clout.'

Winters raised his eyebrows, looked at her sidewise. 'I think I'll take that as a compliment . . . for the moment. "Clout" how, specifically?'

'You got a whole spaceplane diverted.'

'I did?'

'Oh, come on, Mr Winters!' She gave him a look that she hoped wasn't too exasperated. 'You were on the link to my dad early yesterday morning . . . and no more than half an hour later, that flight came down two airports away from where it was supposed to be.'

'Mmm,' Winters said, 'interesting, isn't it . . .'

His attention was on the little brown bird again. 'Go *away*,' he said, 'it's summer, can't you see that? Come back in October.'

Maj held her peace for the moment. After a breath or so, Winters turned back to her and smiled, just slightly. 'Well,' he said, 'just so you know. *I* didn't divert that plane. But there *was* an air marshal on it,' he said as Maj was opening her mouth. 'On the spaceplanes, there always are. And I shoot with the air marshals and some of the FBI and Secret Service guys, once a month or so. This fellow knows me . . . and I was able to convince him to go have a word with the pilot and convince *her* that there was a need to land elsewhere. The airline do this kind of thing all the time for much less reason. And when it happens, they're happy enough to send sky-jitneys for the passengers so that everyone gets where they need to be on time.'

Maj nodded. 'You were that sure that someone was going to try to intercept Laurent . . .'

'Not *that* sure,' Winters said. 'Let's just say that, after talking to your father, I didn't see any harm in throwing a wrench into the works, one that could possibly be mistaken for an accident. Assuming, of course, that there *were* "works." And I think it's safer to assume that there might have been. Some of the people we're dealing with here . . . are not nice.' The grimness of his expression belied the casual phrasing.

'So Laurent's father is pretty important,' Maj said.

'Not politically. No, I take that back. We're not sure how important he might be, politically. Scientifically, there's not much doubt he's irreplaceable. But either way, your father was very concerned . . . and let's just say that there are people who take your father's opinions seriously. Me, for one.'

This was one of those things that Maj was still getting used to, and still occasionally finding hard to understand. She was uncertain exactly what it was her father had to do with Net Force, and he had not been very forthcoming about details.

'Anyway,' Winters said, 'how's Laurent doing?'

'He's okay,' Maj said. 'He's out with Dad at the park, running.'

Winters raised his eyebrows. 'I would have thought he might still be sleeping,' he said. 'Jet lag, or just general fatigue . . .'

'Not a chance. He was in here not twenty minutes ago, looking terrific. You'd think he hadn't just come six thousand miles at all. It's *abnormal*.' Maj grimaced – she always suffered terribly from jet lag, especially traveling east to west. 'Or just unfair.'

Winters made a rueful face. 'I know someone like that,' he said. 'His mother's a Nobel Prize winner in medicine – I think she must have fed him some magic potion when he was a baby . . . or just passed on a hereditary ability to ignore time zones. He flies halfway around the world and it doesn't even make a dent in him. Makes me sick just to think about it.' He laughed a little. 'But anyway, I see that you took the opportunity, while he was out of the way, yadayadayada . . .'

'Uh, yes.'

The little brown bird was back at the feeder again – Winters looked at it with a resigned expression. 'So, Maj,' Winters said. 'Is he a problem, this kid?'

'Not at all,' she said. 'Very nice, in fact. Maybe he acts a little old for his age.'

'It wouldn't be strange,' Winters said, rather quietly, as if more to himself than to her. 'It's not exactly a peaceful environment he's been growing up in, though superficially it may look that way. There's a lot of stress . . . a lot of fear. And it's going to be worse for him, now that some of the pressure's off.'

'He's pretty worried about his dad,' Maj said. 'Though he's trying to cover it up.'

'He has reason to be worried,' Winters said. 'How much has your dad told you?'

'Most of it,' Maj said, feeling it smarter not to be too specific.

Winters nodded, and to Maj's disappointment, refused to be drawn on the subject. 'The country from which he's been taken,' Winters said, 'is not exactly a friendly one.

129

They've been smarting under technology and trade sanctions for a long time, and it's not a situation that's likely to change. They will not take this lying down.' He paused. 'I think your father may have mentioned that some extra security is in the offing . . .'

'Yeah.'

'Good. I'm thinking about what else we can do. Meantime, keep an eye on Laurent. I wouldn't let him run around town by himself.'

'It hadn't occurred to me. Anyway, he doesn't seem interested in that . . . he's a lot more interested in our Net setup.'

Winters grinned a little. 'Yes, I would expect he might be . . . the Net back where he comes from isn't anywhere near as involved as ours. The government there keeps a pretty tight stranglehold on communications generally. It wouldn't do to have the people get any clear idea of how much greener the grass is on the other side.'

Maj made a face. 'Well, I'm trying to break him in gently. Not that it's easy . . . he wants to dive right in. When we finished a six-hour battle last night, he wanted to just jump right back in again as soon as he'd gone to the bathroom.'

'I just bet. Well, again, keep an eye on him – you wouldn't want him to overdo it.'

'That's what his dad said.'

'Oh?'

'To my dad, yeah. He wants to spend some time helping Nick find his way through our Net when he gets here, apparently.'

'A wise parent,' Winters said, and leaned back at the chair, looking at the brown bird, which steadfastly refused to notice that no amount of pecking at the feeder was producing any food.

'You don't suppose . . .' Maj blinked, trying to sort out a sudden new thought.

'What?'

'That his dad hid anything important in his son's Net space when he had it cloned here . . .'

Winters paused visibly, then gave Maj an approving look. 'That's the first thing we checked,' he said. 'No.'

Maj's heart sank a little – she had hoped the idea was original. 'But then I guess,' she said, 'that it would have been the first thing the other side would have thought of, too.'

Winters nodded. 'We moved his material onto one of our secure servers from the one to which it had originally been ported.' he said. 'We've been through that space with a fine-tooth comb, Maj, and there's nothing there but some private writing – not in code – some simple games, and some schoolwork. Though your boy's quite a linguist.'

'Yeah,' Maj said. 'I think he's been holding back to make me feel less ignorant.'

Winters laughed out loud at that. 'Stings, does it? I'm not surprised. I know a couple of people who have the language gift, and it makes me feel like a dolt when I hear them being so fluent. Never mind . . . I'll have more time to start studying languages when I retire. And your whole life's before you . . . you've got plenty of time.'

'It won't be before me if I stay on here much longer,' Maj said, for her mother suddenly put her head into the kitchen, from the hall, and Maj could see her through one of the doorways in her workspace, mouthing the words which probably translated into something like GET IN THE SHOWER NOW OR YOU'LL BE LATE FOR SCHOOL. 'Mr Winters, thanks for your time. I just wanted to check with you myself.'

'Always pleased to help,' he said, and turned his eyes back to the piles of work on his desk. 'Give a shout if you need me.'

'Right. Off,' Maj said, and Winters' image flicked away to blackness, followed a moment later by her workspace. She was sitting in the kitchen again, looking at her mother.

'The phone company called,' she said. 'I can't believe your father told them anyone here would be conscious at this hour.'

'He was,' Maj said.

'Yes, and look who got to answer the call when it came,' said her mother. 'Well, they're sending their people over this morning. I just hope they'll be gone by the time you get home.' She looked annoyed. Maj suspected this was because her mother, not being able to leave well enough alone, would stand over the installers and watch everything they did all day, and then afterwards complain that she had lost a day's work. There were few things better calculated to fray her temper.

Maj got up, stretched, glanced up at the repeater and did the little interior 'blink' that shut her implant's connection to it down. The workspace behind her went away, leaving her in a kitchen rapidly growing brighter with the new day. 'Yeah, I hope they're gone by then, too,' she said. 'Oh, one thing I have to do before I leave . . . order some sweats for Niko . . .'

'I'll take care of that, honey.'

'Have fun. He takes a size thirty-six sneaker.'

'Is that a real size?' her mother said suspiciously.

Maj made her way down to the shower, chuckling.

Maj spent all that day thinking more about Laurent than about anything else. Her morning went by in a strangely disoriented way, and she had trouble concentrating on her classwork, which was unusual for Maj. She plunged through math and physics with no difficulties, but when she hit history, she found that the Teapot Dome scandal seemed unusually remote. Somehow, the history with which she had been dealing at home, the more recent events of a place thousands of miles away, seemed far more concrete and important. In her house, drinking her tea, was someone who had escaped from that history – a particularly nasty piece of it. *Will he ever go back?* Maj wondered. She couldn't imagine wanting to go back to a place where he and his father had been forced to live in such fear. But at the same time, home was home. *He may even love the place*, Maj thought.

If that was the case, she wondered how he managed it. Maj tended to be very sensitive to the emotional atmosphere around her; a fight or a disagreement in the Green household would make her hair stand on end until it was resolved, and even then she would be twitchy about everything everyone said for a day or so afterwards. *He must have known*, she thought, *that they were watching him and his father all the time. I could never stand something like that.* Yet at the same time, possibly it was something you could get used to, like air pollution.

Laurent certainly didn't seem particularly damaged; though maybe this was simply because he was smart. Intelligence, applied to your daily circumstances, was probably a big help. And it was also possible that Laurent was simply a lot tougher than he looked. His slightly delicate appearance could very well be hiding a much more robust personality that you might expect at first glance.

Nonetheless, Maj fretted about him on and off all day, as if her mother wasn't perfectly capable of taking care of

Laurent while Maj was going about her own business. *He's only thirteen,* she kept thinking. *Yeah,* said a voice from the back of her mind, *a thirteen-year-old who is perfectly capable of being shipped thousands of miles away from his normal life at the drop of a hat, and hardly turning a hair. Maybe you should get used to the idea that there are other people at least as competent as you are, even if they are five or six years younger . . .*

But the end of the school day still couldn't come soon enough for Maj. She felt antsy enough to take the local bus home from her high school and walk the two blocks to the house, rather than walking the whole two miles as she preferred to. The last few steps, the last half block or so, she found herself hurrying, and she took the steps up to the front door nearly at a run.

But when she bounced in the door and looked around, everything was quiet. She wandered down the hall, and saw that her mother's office door was slightly open. Her mother was sitting quietly with her hands folded in her lap. 'Mom?' Maj said softly.

Her mother looked over her shoulder, stretched, and yawned. 'Oh,' she said, 'you're back. I wasn't expecting you for another hour yet.'

'This late in the year,' Maj said, 'there's not as much to do as usual . . .'

Her mother looked at her with barely concealed amusement. 'I would have thought,' she said, 'it might have more to do with our guest.'

Maj gave her mother her own version of what her mother described as 'an old-fashioned look.'

'Oh,' Maj said, 'I don't know.' But she wandered further down the hall before her mother could get any more of her guesses right.

'Nice try, honey. He's on line,' her mother called after her. 'In the den.'

'Why does this not surprise me?' Maj said softly as she turned back to her mother's office and leaned against the door. 'Are the phone people done?'

'With the concrete part of the installation, yes,' her mom said. 'They said we might lose service once or twice this afternoon before business hours are done – it seems they have to do some tweaking at the exchange. It shouldn't affect us too much, though. I wouldn't start anything vital right now, that's all.'

'Wasn't planning to.'

Maj wandered down the hall again and looked in the den door, saw Laurent sitting there quietly in the implant chair. The Muffin was sitting in his lap.

Maj smiled a little, and went into the kitchen. She dumped her bookbags and the light jacket she had brought home from school with her, rooted around in the fridge briefly for some milk and a peach, and sat down at the table to line her own implant up with the double over the sink.

From her own workspace she opened the transit door and looked through into the Muffin's. Sure enough, in the midst of the ancient Cambrian rain forest, all waving with giant horsetail ferns and clubmosses, there was Laurent, with a crowd of dinosaurs sitting or standing around him, while the Muffin sat a little elevated on a nearby rock and read to them all.

' "Ay," Puck said. "I'm sorry we lost him out of Old England—" '

Laurent looked up at the slight rustling the dinosaurs made at Maj's approach. He was wearing the new sweats Maj's mother had ordered for him, and looked extremely relaxed.

'All right, you guys,' Maj said, 'shove over . . .'

She pushed a couple of the larger tyrannosaurs out of the way and sat down on the grass next to Laurent, composing herself for the Muffin to resume.

'I was nearly done,' Muf said with some dignity. 'You almost missed everything.'

'Well, go on,' Maj said. 'I'll just have to fill in the blanks. It'll be suppertime soon, and you'll need to wash up. But I'd love to sit here and listen to you finish this first.'

It took about another twenty minutes for the Muffin to plow through to the end of that chapter of *Rewards and Fairies*. Maj and Laurent kept quite still through this – the fierceness of the Muffin's concentration was impressive, and none of the dinosaurs dared to move. Finally, when she was done and closed the book, Laurent applauded a little. The Muffin beamed at him.

'You are very young to be reading that,' he said. 'You're doing very well.'

'I'm not *that* young,' said the Muffin, with the air of a grand dame explaining that she wasn't that old. 'Daddy started reading when he was three. So, what else do you want me to read you?'

'Nothing right now, Muffaletta,' Maj said. 'Mom is going to want to give you supper, and then Daddy will be home.'

'Oh, good,' the Muffin said. 'I'll come back later, then.' She put down the book, and vanished.

Maj and Laurent looked at each other with amusement. 'She really is reading above her age level,' Maj said, 'but it's traditional in the family. Have you read that one before?'

He shook his head. 'It was not familiar.'

'Kipling,' Maj said. 'It's never too late. I'll lend you a paper copy.'

'They would not have let us have such literature at home,' Laurent said, leaning back and looking up at one of the dinosaurs. 'It has kings in it.'

'Presidents, too,' said Maj, 'of wicked foreign countries. That part did, anyway.'

He made an amused snorting sound which reminded Maj, somehow, of her father. 'Yes, we are always warned about the dangers of dealing with decadent Westerners.'

'Decadent,' Maj said, and sighed. 'I wish I had time to be decadent. Lying around doing nothing, you mean, eating chocolates and making a lot of money?'

'That is always the kind of picture I had in my mind,' Laurent said.

Maj laughed. 'Well, you can lose it. I don't know anyone who does that. Though there's a lot of chocolate in my life, I admit that.' She thought she might as well be honest about it, because whenever her brother showed up, *he* certainly would be. One of his less desirable nicknames for Maj was 'Miss Hershey of 2025.'

'But I know some government people, and they don't seem to have time to do anything but work like dogs all day.'

'Oppressing people, my government would say.'

Maj snorted, definitely a copy of her father's sound of derisive amusement. 'You want oppression, take a look at my dad when I tell him I need new clothes,' she said. 'If I'd known there was a way to get the kind of results you seem to be getting, I would have started pretending to be an escapee from your part of the world a long time ago.'

Laurent's grin acquired a slightly sad edge, and he didn't reply.

'I don't suppose,' Maj said, 'there's been any news about your dad . . .'

He shook his head. 'Nothing yet,' he said. And he sighed. 'There are moments when it seems like all this is some kind of dream. A moment ago, just a day or two ago, we were sitting in the apartment, and he said to me, "Lari, time to go now. But one glass of tea before we go." It was the way he said it – it was not going to be just another walk up to the train to go to school. And I said, "*Now?*" and he said, "Ten minutes." Then everything started to move very fast . . .'

Laurent made the snort this time. 'Now all of a sudden here I am in America . . . and I have flown with the Group of Seven against the Archon's Black Arrows . . . and bought clothes without even trying them on—'

'Do they fit?'

'They fit fine.' He laughed out loud at that. 'It is just all so strange. Like another planet.'

Maj thought that his was the world that sounded like another planet – but that was not anything she would have said to him out loud.

'And the Muffin,' he said, with affection. 'Children are not so friendly to strangers, at home. When they meet you, you can see them looking at you and wondering, *Is this person safe?* For we are told from very young that our country is full of spies and saboteurs who want to overturn our good government and put something worse in its place.'

Like what? Maj thought, another reaction she would not have spoken out loud.

'And so you always look at the person and think, *They always told us, anybody could be an enemy . . .*'

'And people from my side of the world,' Maj said, 'definitely.'

Laurent looked at her with a rather dry expression. 'We

also learn young,' he said, 'not to necessarily believe everything they tell us. Or at least some of us do. You are certainly not my enemy. Nor the Muffin.'

'I imagine your president would say we were, though,' Maj said.

Laurent swallowed. 'I think,' he said, 'that my president would also say that my father is a traitor who has sold out to the imperialists, and other things that are not true.' He shook his head. 'A scientist, yes. But I think my father saw that something wrong was happening, that he had invented something that was going to be good, originally, and now was going to be made bad . . . Sorry, I don't have the vocabulary for this.'

'Are you kidding?' Maj said. 'I wish I spoke Romanian like you speak English. All I can do at the moment is sort of stagger around in Greek and German and a little French, and my accent makes grown men cry.'

Laurent smiled at the image. Behind him, a stegosaur lay down with a grunt. 'I think, though,' he said, 'that Popi decided he couldn't do it any more. That he had to stop or it would be too late. I would see him sitting home, sometimes, looking sad . . . as if something had gone so wrong. It hurt me that he couldn't talk about what was the matter. But we *couldn't* talk about it . . . not even when we would go out to the lakes, out west, to go fishing sometimes. You can never tell when somebody is listening. And if you're important, they listen more, not less . . .'

'He must have had ways of telling you, though,' Maj said, her heart wrung by the thought of not being able to openly tell your family what was going on in your head. She knew there were people who probably would think she was out of her mind, but this was how she had been raised – some occasional shouting and stamping, yes, but no uncertainty about where you stood. '*Somehow* or other . . .'

'When it was very important, he would write me notes,' Laurent said, with that dry smile. 'He would leave them on the kitchen table. Always face down . . .'

The image, and what it implied, left Maj speechless for a few seconds. 'But it sounds like you don't know a lot about what he was doing,' she said.

Laurent shook his head. 'He didn't think it was good for me to know too much. It is too easy to become . . . useful . . .'

'A tool,' Maj said. She shivered, though the forest was tropical.

'I know in a general way,' Laurent said. 'He was building micromachines that could walk around inside you and repair cellular damage. Or disassemble tumors, cell by cell. They would have been wonderful things. But one evening he left a note on my pillow, face down. It said, *I am not going to let them make me a murderer. You are going to leave soon, and I will be right behind you.*'

'And here you are,' Maj said.

'Yes,' Laurent said. 'But where is *he?*'

She had no answers for him.

'It is foolish,' he said. 'But I wish, now, that I had taken longer to drink the tea, and look at him . . .'

Around them the ancient forest suddenly split at the seams, leaving Maj sitting at the table and blinking.

'Uh oh,' she said.

'There it goes,' her mother said from down the hall. 'I hope you weren't doing anything important.'

Maj refused to comment. A moment or so later, Laurent wandered in. 'Did I do something wrong?' he said.

'No, it was the repair guys, they're still fiddling with the lines,' Maj said.

'Good. I would not like to think I messed up your sim somehow. I would very much like to fly again later . . .'

Maj gave him an amused look. 'Yeah,' she said, 'I think that can be arranged. Meanwhile, come on, let's see what the fridge wants us to eat before its use-by date.'

Laurent blinked. 'It is going to tell us what to *eat?* I am not sure I approve.'

'See that, you're getting decadent already,' Maj said, and pulled the refrigerator door open. 'Let's graze. But if you don't want to hear this thing get really ugly, stay away from the butter . . .'

Six

The spaceplane was much more comfortable than it had any right to be, even in coach, and the Major sat there by the window, looking out at the curvature of the earth, and could feel little except a vague sense of offense that such an experience should routinely be denied to her people. The western countries could blather all they liked about the danger of terrorism to the planes, and their right to attempt to negate it by strictly controlling access to them. It was all finally about keeping the 'banana republics' in their place – keeping down small independent-minded countries whose only sin was disagreeing with the big and powerful ones, refusing to dance to their tune. The Major disliked having to travel on forged documents – she was pleased with who she was, and with the nation which had raised her, despite all the attempts of the big countries to interfere, in its own moral and economic tradition. Still, sometimes work made you do things you didn't care for . . . and right now, getting the job done was much more important than indulging her personal preferences.

Besides, there was always the matter of promotions to consider.

She glanced up one more time at the light for Net cabin at the end of the 'coach' area – still red. She glanced one more time at the screen in front of her, still blathering in 3D and full color about some inexplicable service it wanted her to buy. In one corner of the stereo display (rather annoyingly good for such a small one) was a red digit 2, blinking steadily. Two people ahead of her in the queue. *The sheer spoiled impatience of these people,* she thought. *Only three hours in this thing, and they have to be indulging themselves on the Net half the time? Why don't they just stay home hooked up to their damned machines if they can't do without their drug for that long?* Especially when people who really needed to use the Net, like her, were kept waiting.

And as for what they did with it . . . well. The Net could have been a wonderful tool for education and commerce, but like anything else sourced in the western countries, it had become a tool for endless hucksterism, a way to make jobs for more people selling things that people didn't really need, services simply designed to make you more lazy or stupid than you already were . . . a goal which she suspected the western democracies fully supported, since they kept themselves in power by the votes of the few human beings being energetic enough to haul themselves out of their houses to a polling place, but still naïve or dim enough to believe that their voices made a difference. It could have been an endearing illusion, if the countries encouraging it in their citizens had not been so overwhelmingly, unfairly powerful, sitting on coffers and arsenals fattened by centuries of this operation.

Indeed, she thought as yet another screaming, out-of-control child ran down the aisle nearest her with its parent in leisurely pursuit, there was a truth there which the democracies were missing – one which would have made them more powerful still if they had ever gotten to grips with it. Individuals might be clever, or useful, but people in the mass, the great enfranchised mobs that constituted the North American and European democracies, *people* were stupid. If you really meant to keep your working population well fed, productive, and obedient, the best way to manage this was to completely ignore their ideas about how to run a country – since mostly they didn't have any, or only ones which had never been thought through. Tell them how it should be done, *show* them how it should be done . . . and if they complained, if they didn't like the way things were run, let them go somewhere else. After you had gotten anything out of them which made a fair return for the money you had spent raising them, of course.

This last part of her viewpoint was possibly heretical, and not one that she would ever have shared. The Major doubted that the President thought it fair that anyone on whom the State had spent funds should ever be allowed to leave except for the most pressing reasons, or possibly any reason at all . . . and certainly not just because they felt like it. That being, of course, the whole reason for this whole exercise.

The stereo display began showing a rechanneled version of some ancient film, and the Major sat back in her seat and sighed; and the digit in the corner of the display turned to '1' as a woman came out of the Net booth and a man went in. *I could almost find it in my heart to feel sorry for poor Darenko,* she thought, *when we finally force him out of hiding. Except that there will probably not be much left to be sorry for. Once a man has betrayed him, especially a man who has so much to be grateful for, and a man of such gifts, Cluj is not the sort to readily forgive.* And under the circumstances, she could understand it. How a man could do all the work necessary to lay a mighty weapon in his nation's hand, an invaluable tool – and then, with the work almost finished, simply get up and flee . . . It was insanity at best, and treachery at worst. In either case, putting the man out of his misery was the best and quickest option. And in the case of treachery, doing it as publicly as possible was always a good idea. *Every now and then,* she thought, *the people, stupid as they are, will understand an example set before them if it's nasty enough. If they—*

The digit '1' turned to '0' and began flashing as the man came out of the booth. To the man sitting reading beside her, the Major said, 'Excuse me—' and got up to slip past him, heading for the booth. She sidestepped skilfully around yet another child plunging down the aisle and into the booth. Inside, she leaned back against the 85-degree support couch that leaned forward from the wall, lined up her implant, and when the temporary workspace came up around her, set it for scramble and gave it the necessary address.

She waited for the encryption protocols to come up and breathed out in annoyance. *They can't even discipline their children,* she thought. *Here they are running loose like so many hooligans, free to annoy anyone they like. You wouldn't see this kind of behavior at home, our children know that they'd—*

She found herself looking at the Minister, Bioru, in his office. 'Sir,' she said and, not being in uniform, did not salute. 'I had thought I would be talking to—'

'I intercepted the call. We have had some movement, Major.'

Her heart started to pound. 'Has he been found?'

'Not as yet. But one of his associates has begun telling us what we want to know.'

She had wondered when they would start getting results. Questioning was always such a tricky business – those who seemed most potentially resistant sometimes cracked immediately through fear or overimaginativeness, while others who seemed least likely to put up a fight sometimes produced astonishing amounts of resistance, either due to high pain thresholds or plain stubbornness. In all cases it took a professional to work out how much force to apply, and in what form – and there were too many chances for accidents, as she'd seen. She had been dreading another. 'I am very glad to hear that,' she said.

'The details,' said Bioru, looking grim, 'are rather less cause for joy. Darenko's work was nearly complete, the final stage of his construction almost ready for delivery. But apparently he had reservations which he did not share with us about the purposes to which his work would be put. As if he had any right to such.' The frown got blacker. 'Apparently he has been feeding our agent on his team false progress reports for some while . . . and, during that time, he has been both sabotaging his other associates' work, and destroying or undoing work which he himself has done. Various "partial" prototypes of the microps have been destroyed, or rendered useless in ways which were undetectable until someone actually tried to activate the mechanisms. And we have none of the fully functional models left, none at all. Darenko destroyed them before he left, possibly with something as simple as a Net-borne command to their programming centers.'

He sat going through his papers, and that terrible smile appeared again, so that the Major shivered. 'Thousands of hours' worth of his and his colleagues' work,' he said, 'all gone in a moment . . . Though it was not a momentary act. The man must have been planning this for a long while . . . the worst kind of treason. He worked until the project was almost ready, then destroyed the active prototypes. All but a few . . .'

'Where are they?' she whispered, shocked by the enormity of what Darenko had done. 'Does he have them?'

He glanced up at the Major again, and that smile got more feral, something that she had not believed could happen. 'No,' he said, 'but someone else does.'

She opened her mouth, closed it again. 'The boy,' she said.

Bioru nodded. 'Darenko was not so indifferent to the value of his work,' he said, 'that he was willing to simply throw it away. The boy is carrying fully enabled microps in his body. They are so small that it would have been no trouble at all to simply give them to him in a glass of milk. To judge by what the associate has told us, they are now floating around in his bloodstream doing general maintenance work, their "default" programming – stripping cholesterol off the interiors of his arteries, killing passing germs, and taking apart noxious compounds like lactic acid and so forth.' The smile fell away. 'Major, I do not care for the idea that a weapon which could do our country great good in its unending battle against spies and enemies inside and outside is presently meandering around the circulatory system of a traitor's son, protecting him from the ill effects of Western junk food!'

'I will recover him immediately,' she whispered.

'No, you will *not*,' Bioru said.

The Major's eyes widened.

'There is something that must be done first,' the Minister said. 'I had some hint of this material, but I was unwilling to go on the record until it had been confirmed, and this is why I told you earlier that you were to be ready to pick the boy up *on signal* but not before. You will not be the only one receiving a signal.'

'The microps,' she said.

'Yes. The associate has been most forthcoming as regards the activation codes and the necessary methods for instructing the microps in what their new role will be. We will activate them and set them to work on the boy's central nervous system – with predictable results. We will make sure the father knows about this. We have a good guess, now, where he is and how he is equipped – but there is no need to go digging him out. In perhaps thirty-six hours from the microps' activation he will come to us without hesitation. Otherwise, if he *does* hesitate—' Bioru shrugged. 'We will not countermand the routine the microps have been running, and it will really be too bad for the boy. I have seen the slides from the test animals,' he added, turning over some more paperwork, and glancing at a photocopy of something the Major could not clearly see from this angle. 'There was apparently a mistake in one of the commands given in an early series of tests. After this particular "erroneous" command is given to the microps, the resemblance of the subject brain at the end of the process to one which has been infected with one of the spongiform encephalopathies is quite remarkable. "Sponge" is definitely the operative term.'

'But if the father should not respond in time, if the boy should die—?'

Bioru shrugged again. 'Morgues are routinely even more lax in security terms than hospitals,' he said. 'We can as easily harvest the microps from a corpse as we can from a live body. More easily – corpses do not need anesthesia. Either way, with the boy alive or dead, we will have no problems with Doctor Darenko in future. If the boy survives, we will keep young Laurent as a hostage to further work by his father. If he does not, we will at least have recovered the microps, and can pass them on to some other expert more loyal than Darenko for development.'

The Major nodded. 'When will the activation happen?' she said.

'We are still working on the details,' Bioru said. 'We think Darenko may have warned his son to stay off the Net, fearing that someone might work out how to send an activation or reprogramming burst to the microps.' The smile began to grown again. 'In any case, the warning seems not to be having much effect. Granted, the boy has not yet ventured anywhere much except the Greens' household Net – unfortunately this has become inaccessible from outside. They seem to have had some work done on their bandwidth just now, and the work included some unusual one-way traffic protocols. It seems from the phone company's records that the good professor is paranoid about colleagues stealing the articles he writes for his various journals.' Briefly that smile became merely malicious. 'Other than that, the only other place he has been is this' – he peered at another piece of paper – ' "Cluster Rangers" entertainment which the daughter seems presently to favor.'

'My department has registered with that server,' the Major said. 'Their registration should be going through shortly.'

'It has already gone through,' said Bioru. 'However, the boy has not yet ventured back in. Once he is in active "gameplay," we will be ready to send the reprogramming burst. After that, it will take no more than eighteen hours for him to begin showing symptoms, and at that point we will notify the father, through public media to which he has access, of his son's condition. If he cooperates, we will send a "stop" burst and hold the damage to the boy's system at whatever level it has reached when Darenko turns himself in. *Then* you will bring the boy home. By then he will probably be ill enough to be taken to the hospital . . . and that is the point at which, if you have not already found an opportunity to move, you can easily do so. No one questions an ambulance crew answering a summons to fetch a sick child. After that, a quick trip to our embassy, and he will come home the same night in the diplomatic pouch, under seal, where none of the local police or security forces can touch him. It will hardly be the first time our embassy has designated a carrier large enough to contain a person as the "pouch." Notice is unlikely to be taken . . . and even if it is, there is nothing any of the various intelligence or security forces can do – they will not dare interfere with diplomatic immunity.'

The Major smiled too, now, just slightly. 'I will see to the details.'

'I doubt there will be much in the way of interference from the Green family until it is too late,' said Bioru. 'The only sensitive part of this operation will be happening when they will be too distracted by the symptoms to suspect the cause, let alone to delve far into it. However, if there should be any interference—'

'The father's ties to Net Force . . .'

'Mere cronyism, as far as I can tell,' said Bioru. 'He seems to lecture to their people a great deal. He is not an active operative, and they are hardly likely to go out on a limb for him. Do what you have to do to get the boy, Major. This matter is too important for me to enjoin you against deadly force. If this weapon falls into the hands of our enemies – even of some of our present allies – many of our people in the field could die as a result. What is the saying? "Do unto others as they would do unto you – and do it first"?'

She nodded. 'I will take care of it.'

'See that you do,' Bioru said, and vanished.

She was left in the unornamented black workspace of the booth, sweating slightly. The Major sighed, smoothed her hair back into place and opened the door.

Yet another small child, a boy of about four, barreled full tilt into her legs. She caught him. 'Uh, oh,' she said, 'look out, sweetheart!' – and pushed him off gently in the direction of his mother, who was coming down the aisle after him.

Then she walked back to her seat, smiling gently, and thing about young Laurent.

'Look,' Maj said. 'At least give it some thought.'

The Group of Seven were in session later that evening, sitting around in Kelly's present workspace, a bizarre multistory log cabin located in some mythical backwoods surrounded by mountains high enough to make Everest feel slightly inferior. Kelly changed workspace styles the way some people changed their underwear, so the Group made it a habit to meet regularly at his place, just to see what he was up to – mostly never the same thing twice.

The Great Hall of this particular cabin was scattered with animal hides which would have been extremely politically incorrect if they had been genuine. However, they weren't, and some of them were simply hypothetical. Mairead was presently curled up on one of the five huge sofas, absently petting one of the pelts, an amazing thing streaked in midnight blue and silver. 'This is really pretty,' she had commented when they first came in, 'they should make an animal to go with it . . .'

Now, though, she looked across to Maj, who was sitting on the sofa closest to the huge open fireplace. Maj had always been a sucker for fires, and she was presently gazing into the flames, estimating idly that you could probably roast a whole cow in this fireplace, assuming you had a block and tackle to lift the cow.

'Look,' Mairead said. 'It's not that he's not a nice kid. He is. But I'm just not sure how committed he is to simming.'

'Lots of people think it's simming they're interested in, when what they really want is to be a fighter jockey,' Kelly said. 'Nothing wrong with that. But it's not what we do. If we start diluting the purpose of the group, adding people who're going to pull it in different directions, it's going to start coming to pieces. I've seen that kind of thing too often before.'

'Yeah,' said Chel.

Shih Chin frowned. 'Kel, it's easy to say that. But what about the other side of the argument? Do we want to shut ourselves off entirely from new blood, good people, just because we're not sure they fit some narrow little definition of our own purpose? Don't we have the room to grow a little?'

'Yeah, but—'

It had been going on in this vein for the better part of three-quarters of an hour now, and Maj felt like getting up, creating a can of spray paint, and graffiti-ing right across the biggest of the log walls, YOU ARE ALL UNCLEAR ON THE CONCEPT. That might at least get their attention. However, it was considered bad form to trash others' workspaces, no matter how sorely one was tempted – though there had been the time Chel had

purposely built the Castle of the Sugar Plum Fairy, and
everyone had lost their composure in unison—

That *was* unison, though, and the occasional outbreaks
of unison were one of the things that made the Group of
Seven worth sticking with. Maj sighed.

'*Guys*,' she said.

There was a lull in the argument. This was not necessarily
a good sign – there had been several so far, to no effect.

'Look,' she said. 'I'm not asking for an answer today.
I'm not even sure I *want* an answer today, whether
everybody has one or not. I just felt the need to let you
know that Niko really likes what we are doing. He thinks
he might be good at it . . . and he'd like to "try out." He
wants a chance to get to know you better. And possibly to
fly with you on a regular basis, if possible. But otherwise,
he just would really like to fly with us sometimes . . . for
now.'

'How long is "now"?' Chel said.

That was where Maj had gotten stuck the last time, for
she was unwilling to let them know or guess too much
about what was going on. 'His folks may be moving over
here,' she said. 'They'll be coming to visit for a while – his
dad, will, anyway – but I'm not sure how long it's going to
last. I'm not even dead sure it's going to be permanent.'

'Not that it matters when we're all virtual,' Mairead
said.

Yeah, but some of us are more virtual than others. Laurent
had briefly shown her his small bare ported-over workspace – just blackness with text and pictures hanging in it –
and she had been at pains to cover up her embarrassment
for him in a hurry, and to show him how to build it into an
environment he could sit in and get comfortable with. He
was a fast learner, but it was still going to take him time to

get used to all the 'special effects' now available to him, things that everyone else here had long taken for granted.

'What is likely to be affected is how often he can get in,' Maj said, 'after the immediate present. This is sort of a quiet time for him.' She sighed. 'Look, do I have to spell it out? He's lonely. You guys made him welcome.'

Shih Chin made an aggrieved face. '*Some* of us called him "*Goulash*".'

'He didn't mind,' Bob said.

'No,' Maj said, 'he didn't. He's a good-natured kid, for someone so young.'

'There's that, too,' Del said, a little dubiously. 'I mean, it's nothing personal, we were all thirteen once—'

'Some of us may have done it twice,' Mairead muttered into the fur she was still stroking, looking sideways at Sander.

There was some muted snickering about this – the juvenile nature of Sander's sense of humor was legendary in the Group.

Maj refused to be distracted. 'In this case,' she said, 'I'm not sure how much chance he's had to be thirteen in the first place. He's had a bad time of it at home. I'm not going to get into details. There has been family stuff going on for him, and he's had to grow up fast. A lot of work, not much play, and not a whole lot of smart people who're also nice to play with.'

' "Play," ' Sander said, a little archly.

' "When I became a man," ' said Bob suddenly, in a quoting tone of voice, ' "I put aside the concerns of a child, including the fear of looking childish, and the desire to seem very grown up." '

Everyone looked at him. 'Well,' he said, only a little defensively, 'we're old enough to cut each other some slack when we act underage, aren't we?' He looked at Sander. 'We can surely make a little allowance for someone who's a little *older* than his age.' He looked at Maj. 'Does he have any previous simming experience at all?'

'You're not going to believe this,' Maj said, 'but he had never even *been* in a sim before last night.'

'God,' said Shih Chin, in complete astonishment. 'Talk about deprivation.'

'It's not like they don't have the Net over there, Maj,' Kelly said. 'What was the problem? Financial or something?'

'I think maybe so,' she said. 'Look, guys, please, there's no need for any "final" decisions. But he'd like to fly with us a couple of times, get the feel for what we're doing. If it becomes obvious that he really *is* just a rocket jockey, I'll take him aside and show him where better to practice the art. But, meantime . . .'

There was some silence. 'When are we scheduled up next?' Bob said.

'You're the squadron leader. You don't have the schedule?'

'Schedule,' Kelly said to his workspace. With a flourish of trumpets, there appeared in midair before them a meter-long parchment scroll supported at each end by a small flying cherub. The parchment unrolled, showing a Day-Timer page made large.

Mairead gave this apparition a look. '*Very* rococo,' she said. 'Obviously you're unconcerned that Della Robbia might sue.'

'Wednesday,' Kelly said.

'That's the old schedule. I can't do Wednesday,' Bob said. 'I have jazz class that night.'

'Tuesday?'

'Cripes, that's tomorrow already,' Sander said.

'No good for me,' Mairead said. 'My turn to cook at

home.' She looked at Sander. 'And by the way, what about those chillis you were going to get for me?'

'Uh, I forgot. Tuesday's out for me, though.'

'I can do Tuesday,' Bob said.

'Me, too,' Kelly said. 'Who else can't do Tuesday?'

Maj searched her mind. 'I'm okay, I think.'

'I'm in,' Del said.

'Me too,' Robin said. 'I have a half day. What time?'

Time zones . . . Maj thought. 'Six o'clock eastern?'

'I think I'm going to have to pass,' Mairead said. 'I have a ton of homework that night, and then a six a.m. bus the next morning. Sorry. I'll come in the next time.'

They played the 'schedule game' for a few minutes more. Finally Maj agreed to meet Del and Robin and Bob on Tuesday night at seven. 'We can show Niko some of the underpinnings of what we're doing,' she said. 'See if he catches fire at the idea of building one of these from scratch rather than just playing in someone else's sim.'

'Fair enough,' Bob said. 'We'll report off to the rest of the Group. If this doesn't work out, though, Maj . . . even if he *is* your cousin or whatever . . .'

'I'll let him down gently,' she said. 'I'm not going to ride you guys about this. I appreciate what you're doing, anyway.'

'Okay,' Bob said. 'Kelly, for cripe's sake will you get those things out of there? They're creating a draft.' He waved one hand at the cherubs.

'Begone, bugs,' Kelly said. They and the 'parchment' vanished.

'Okay,' Bob said. 'Down to work.'

In the air in the midst of them appeared the wireframe model of the Arbalest fighter. It rotated in three axes, its usual 'presentation' spin, and then fleshed itself over in black mirror alloy and settled in 'plan view,' horizontal to them. 'Right,' Bob said. 'I think we can get rid of any worries about the camber of the wings, because they worked just fine. Now, here's what we might look at next . . .'

Maj breathed out a sigh of relief and leaned in to see what Bob was going to propose. *One less thing to worry about,* she thought. *We'll see how Tuesday goes . . .*

In the next room, or six thousand miles away, depending on how one looked at it, Laurent stood in the apartment he shared with his father, looking around him.

It was not really such a bad place. *A workspace,* he thought. He was going to have to learn the terms that they used here. Maj had been able to take a few minutes to show him how to manipulate the bare space into which his own files had been moved.

It was still all so strange . . . He was unused to experiencing virtual life as anything but dry text, flat or stereo images, everything a little remote and forbidding, concepts and pictures appearing in darkness and disappearing into it again . . . with always the hint that somewhere, out in that darkness, someone was listening to you, waiting for you to say something wrong.

It had been as unlike the waiting, welcoming darkness of the *Cluster Rangers* universe as anything could have been. *That,* Laurent thought, *is the way virtuality always should have been. Friendly. Oh, naturally there will always be things that are scary – nobody wants to be protected all the time. But there's more than enough of that in the real world. Why does the virtual world have to be the same way . . . hard and chilly and always so determined and serious? Why won't the government at home let people have at least this kind of thing . . . this room to let their imaginations run free a little?*

Of course, that might be the reason, right there. *Free. Imaginations*, stimulated, in constant use, could be dangerous things. *The* most *dangerous thing*, he remembered his father saying. *Every good thing there is, started as someone's dream. So did nearly every bad thing that man has made – as a dream that went wrong, or one that was purposely twisted into a nightmare from the beginning. None of them could happen without imagination. It is the thing that most frightens people, after enthusiasm. Against the two of them together, there is no defense . . .*

Except, Laurent thought, *when whatever is chasing 'imagination' and 'enthusiasm' down the street has a gun, and they do not . . .*

He sighed and wandered off to the window, looking down onto the little bare courtyard that lay at the back of their house. A hedge bordered it, and there were sidewalks on the other side of the hedge, and to either side were concrete multistory apartment buildings exactly like their own. Off in the distance straight ahead was a line of trees, and far beyond that a shadowy line against the sky, almost the same color as the sky in this weather – the hills of the north. And over those hills . . . the rest of the world, the world he had believed he would never see.

But now all that was changed. This was the world he had given up, the world he would – strangely – now give anything to be standing in again. He would turn around and see his father—

Laurent turned around . . . but the room was empty. Cupboards, the dining-room table, the little kitchenette where the two of them made their meals, the doors leading to each of the two bedrooms, everything white and plain and neat – there it all was. But his father was not there. On the kitchen table was a note, turned face down.

Laurent let out a long breath and went over to the table, stared down at the note. Before she went to take care of her own business, Maj had shown him a little about how to bend his mind against this space, ordering it to manifest visual and tangible links which would hook into other resources on the Net and also make the place look less bare. The standard virtual workspace was endlessly malleable, and would give him, in illusion anyway, anything he wanted.

Laurent pulled out one of the chairs and sat on it, looking around at the cool afternoon light that was filling the apartment. Everything was very quiet. Properly, he knew that he should instruct the program to fill in some background noise, but he was in no hurry about that.

Maj, Laurent thought. She had been very kind to him . . . a lot kinder than she needed to be. The whole Green family had – Mr Green, his father's friend – and the Muffin, who climbed up in Laurent's lap and looked around her to make sure no one was within earshot, and whispered conspiratorially, 'Are you *sure* you aren't my brother?' They *felt* like family – it was almost as if the cover story was trying to come true.

But he was still a little shy with Maj's mother. It was not that she reminded him specifically of his own mother, gone six years now. Those memories were faint already, getting fainter all the time – the memory of a hand touching his shoulder, the echo of a voice, laughing. He was already finding it hard to remember his mother's face, and this troubled him. It felt obscurely like some kind of disloyalty. But you couldn't make your mind remember what it refused to. Sometimes it just let go of things, he thought, because they hurt too much. He shied away from

Maj's mother a little, not because she was unkind, but because if he too freely accepted the kindness, he might be further tempted to forget the touch, the echo, completely . . . and he didn't dare. Besides, there was always the fear lingering at the edge of things, not to get too involved, not to commit yourself . . . because just when you're getting used to it, when you think things might change, it can all be taken away from you again, leaving you emptier than you were to start with.

Laurent sighed, looked toward the closed front door, which led into Maj's workspace. She was elsewhere, he knew. He thought he would invite her in when she was free. But then the idea of what she might think when she looked in here, after being so used to the sumptuous spaces she routinely moved through, began to chill him a little. She would be polite about it. But he knew she would be thinking how poor it all looked, how barren. She would know it wasn't his fault . . . but she would still *think* that. And he had been embarrassed enough lately.

No, let it wait a while, let him find time to do some more work. There was likely to be too much time to work anyway, for a while, until they found his father.

If they found his father . . .

He turned around, then, and made the image. The tall man in the worn dark coat . . . Popi never had a coat that wasn't a little too short for him in the sleeves. He just had unusually long arms and wrists and hands, and they never failed to hang out of the State coats, which were made to averages and not for individuals. Tall and blond, a little hawkish looking, the high cheekbones and the long nose reinforcing the look – but the glasses always adding that last touch of owl, turning the hawk-expression friendly and quizzical. There he was – his father. Laurent turned.

161

The figure standing there was incomplete – it had no face.

I'm forgetting already, Laurent thought, in rising panic. *It's only been a couple of days . . .!* 'I won't! I *won't* forget!' he shouted. '*Go away!*'

When he looked again, the figure was gone.

He stood there, breathing hard, feeling silly for having overreacted. Finally Laurent let out a long breath, a sigh, and reached down to the table, to the note – turned it over.

The other side was blank.

He let it fall.

Laurent got up, then, and turned to the shelf by the window, where he had placed one thing which did not exist in the real apartment. It was a model of an Arbalest fighter – an icon leading to Maj's fighter in her *Cluster Rangers* account. She had, she said, put the 'training wheels' on it for him, so that he could fly it with minimum experience, inside her own simming space.

Laurent decided not to wait. *She'll understand,* he thought, and went over to pick up the model of the fighter. *I really need a break, something to take my mind off . . .*

Say it. *Off the fear.* That your father will never come back, never get out. That they have him in some dark place, and they're doing to him what they did to Piedern's father two years ago, when they caught him handling foreign publications. But what they do this time will be worse, much worse, because your father was one of the special ones . . . and he turned on them. They never forgive that. Never.

Laurent took in a long breath, let it go. Took another breath.

All right, he thought. *Let's get a grip, here. Let's go*

somewhere that the dark is friendly, just for a little while. I won't stay long. I promised I wouldn't overdo it – and Mrs Green will probably have dinner ready in a little while . . . it would be rude to be late.

He put the model of the Arbalest down on the shelf again, and stood there touching it. 'Guest ingress,' he said.

Laurent vanished, leaving the model there by itself, the one black thing in the white room.

Seven

Elsewhere, another room was very small and dark. It had been a coal bin, once, in the cellar of this house, in a time when people still used coal for heating in the cities; its walls were black with soot, and a few forgotten lumps of coal still lay around on the rammed dirt of the floor. The coal-cellar had just one way to the outside, a pair of metal doors at a forty-five degree angle to the stucco of the building. The doors' hinges were long since rusted shut, as was the padlock through the old hasp, connecting them. They had been painted over, for good measure, some time in the last decade, with (in a gesture of optimism) a rustproofing paint. Plainly, from its external appearance, no one could possibly be in here . . . which made it an excellent place to hide.

Armin Darenko sat as comfortably as he could, leaning against the sooty wall, concentrating on the tiny line of light that came to him through those old doors, from a not-quite-painted-over crack on the right hand side of one of them. He had come in a couple of days ago, in the dead of night, through the tunnel in the middle of the floor. His clean clothes were down in that tunnel, now, so as not to become smirched with soot that would draw attention to him when it was time to leave. He knew that time would come in the next few days – his friends were working for him, out there. But that did not stop him from being afraid, as he sat here, and his mind ran in frightened circles like a rat in a particularly inhumane Skinner box, always looking for the cheese and never finding it, and being shocked again and again by the same fear.

He sighed, took a deep breath and tried, for the thousandth time, to break the cycle. Laurent was safe. Of that much he was sure. Laurent was in Alexandria, with the Greens, and was almost certainly coping splendidly. His son had all his mother's old toughness, that ability to deal with what was happening around her and not be more trouble to others than necessary. And he was carrying the silent little helpers which would keep him healthy, protect him by brute force from passing infections against which he might not have been inoculated, keep his system chemistry in kilter and otherwise make themselves useful. Very useful indeed they would be, some day, when they were in the right hands and turned loose to help a suffering world. For the moment, though, Laurent was their unwitting custodian, and in a safe place . . . so the two things which Armin Darenko had been most concerned about were now safe. Now Armin was free to concentrate on getting himself out of this cellar.

Getting in had been easy enough for a man who for a long, long time had considered that there might come a day which called for a sudden departure. Escapes planned at the last moment rarely do well, he knew. So, quietly, Armin had begun, about twenty years ago, keeping his ears open for information which might come in handy eventually. And sure enough, it came. When governments began to change with more than the usual speed, rumors flourished about tunnels under the city. Some of them were just that, rumors – but some turned out to be true. This particular network of tunnels, which apparently went right back to the bad old Ceaucescu days, turned out to exist. They did not lead far – just from cellar to cellar of some of the houses in this part of town – but that fact in itself made them useful, since tunnels which actually led directly to escape would have been found long since and filled in, or blown up. Right now, a simple place to hide was all that Armin wanted in the world.

He had enough food and water to keep him going for a couple of days yet, and a cache under a rock in the nearby park where he could, with the greatest caution and in the dark of night, slip out and get more, if he needed it. He was intent on not going out if he could avoid it, however – not until he heard, on the tiny radio he was carrying, the coded news from the people who had agreed to help get him out. Armin had risked enough going out to the lakes, three days ago, to leave the false trail that he much hoped would concentrate the authorities' search in that direction. It was too much to hope that they would search there for long. They were not stupid people. But even a short distraction would allow the friends who were helping him to complete their own plans. With luck, in a couple of days, maybe less, he would go to join Laurent.

And then life would have to begin again for both of them. He knew the medical community in the States would welcome him. So would others . . . and this time he would have to be more careful than he had been here. It was not as if there were not cruel, venal and evil people in the United States, just as well as here; people who would see, in the delicate and intelligent little machines he had created, a weapon instead of a tool. He would have to work with Martin, and with Martin's friends at Net Force and elsewhere in the intelligence and scientific communities, to find ways to control his creations so that they could not be modified for deadly purposes.

He sighed, alone in the darkness, and knew that it would be an uphill fight, if indeed this purpose could be achieved at all. There was no putting the genie back in the bottle, as the old story had it. It was out now – out walking around the world in his son's body. Soon enough it would be in the lab, being studied by other scientists. And after that . . .

Armin felt around him in the darkness for the plastic bottle of spring water, took a swig, sealed it and put it aside again. At least he had left no working prototypes here. What hurt him most now was the price he suspected that some of the people who had been working with him must be paying. But there comes a time when one must, however reluctantly, weigh lives in one's hand – one's own life, as well as those of others – and decide whether sparing two lives, or five or ten, here and now, is worth losing thousands, perhaps millions, later on. For Armin was not so naïve as to think his invention would stay inside his country's borders if he completed it and turned it over to the government. Cluj desperately needed hard currency. He would sell the microps to anyone who would pay him. Terrorists, intelligence organizations, criminals, common murderers, other countries with better intentions, would all pay well. And chaos would ensue. Soon the negative uses would proliferate, outnumbering the positive ones. No one would know whether what they ate was normal food, or something that could take them apart from the inside – either slowly, molecule by molecule, or very quickly indeed.

Armin's only consolation was that he had managed to destroy all the locally-held records about the section of coding which told the microps how to 'breed,' how to reproduce themselves from raw materials, protein chains and mineral ions, inside their host. He had destroyed not only the code, before he left, but all his notes, and as many of his associates' notes as possible. Not all of them had been accessible . . . but he had made sure that it would be a long, long while before anyone would be able to retro-engineer the microps from the bits and pieces which were all that remained when he had left the laboratory for the last time the other night.

Half his work was done. Now all that remained was to get himself to safety as well. The people who had slowly let him know that they would help him were now busy out there – he would hear from them soon. Most of his time he now spent listening to the little radio on its earphone, amusing himself by judging the tenor of the search for him by the increasing or decreasing shrillness of the announcements about him during the 'crime bulletins.' The rest of the time, he spent thinking about new microps designs, taking refuge in the sweet orderliness of the molecular-level world, where structure and symmetry reigned . . .

. . . And about his son. *Safe, thank God,* he thought; *safe* . . .

In the darkness, he closed his eyes.

The darkness sang to him, and Laurent streaked out through it, laughing. Maj had been right about the Arbalest. It needed very little expertise in handling, in this mode – a normal joystick was enough. 'Right now you're going to be flying it for pleasure, not mastery,' she said, having handed him the icon. 'So there's no harm in letting the game module "read your mind" a little. But don't overdo it. And I wouldn't go into the main game, if I were you. The

169

Archon's people are still drifting around there trying to make trouble, some of them . . . and if you get my fighter shot up, we're going to have words.'

But she had also shown him how to return instantly from the *Cluster Rangers* game to her own simming space . . . and Laurent had not been able to resist. Maj's recreated space, though full of stars and matching the *Cluster Rangers* space closely in terms of astrography and physical laws – this being important for the high-G work – still did not have that subtle, sublime look-and-feel that the original had. He craved the sound of the stars singing, and he was going to have just a little of it, on his own, before coming back to mundane life again.

Listen to me, he thought as he flew up and over the curve of Dolorosa, into that spectacular view. *'Mundane', I am calling her life, after only, what? A day and a half of it? Two days. And a life that any of the other kids at school would kill for – I don't care how high up in the government their fathers are. Look at me! I'm becoming jaded. Decadent.*

He laughed for sheer pleasure as the great arm of the Galaxy spread itself out before him, the sound of it shimmering silvery against the ship's skin, tingling all through him. *This is what virtuality should be like,* Laurent thought, tumbling the Arbalest in its yaw axis so that it turned to face the view of the great heart of the Seraphim Cluster, all those burning jewels spilled out across the night, flaring and fading, flaring and fading again. *I would never have thought the stars could have so many colors,* he thought. He knew the stellar types, but the prosaic letters and numbers did not even hint at this wild treasury of shades and brilliances, set dazzling in the darkness.

It is enough to turn me into an astronomer, Laurent

thought. And a big shiver went through him, hot and cold at once, and then another one, so that he was surprised for a moment, and checked the ship's controls to see if something was wrong with the suit-conditioning system, or the cockpit's own environmental controls. But all the lights were green, so that Laurent laughed again, at himself this time. He tumbled the ship once more to get one last look at that huge arm of the Galaxy, lying draped over a third of the sky, like a blazing banner spread out on some impossible wind—

'Niko?'

Uh-oh, he thought, and tumbled the ship one more time, getting a fix on Maj's hangar and heading for it. 'Coming—'

It was Maj's mother, outside virtual space. It amused Laurent that her family all seemed to leave the option open to talk to each other from inside or outside their various virtualities, no matter what they were doing. 'Do you eat lamb, honey?'

'Lamb? Yes!'

'Oh, good,' she said, invisible but amused. 'An enthusiast. Garlic?'

'We all have to eat garlic,' Laurent said. 'It is required. It keeps the Transylvanians away.'

'Mmm, no comment,' Maj's mother said. 'If I didn't know better, I would have believed you about the cows, too. Are you going to be in there much longer?'

'I am coming out now,' Laurent said. He was landing the Arbalest in Maj's hangar even as he spoke – which was just as well, since the light over one of the hangar's pedestrian doors started flashing, indicating that someone wanted to come in.

'Good,' Maj's mother said. 'Because the Muffin is giving

me grief at the moment that you are not available to be played with.'

'Oh. I will be right out.'

The hangar ceiling was almost finished shutting, and the huge space began to repressurize.

' "Niko",' said Maj's voice in the middle of the air, suggesting that the Muffin was indeed within range, 'what are you doing in there?'

'Just letting the air back in.'

The process finished as he got down onto the floor again. The flashing light over the door turned green, and the door opened. Maj came strolling across the syncrete as Laurent went through the walk-around, which Maj told him was traditional among pilots, to make sure that nothing had fallen off their craft – or if it had, to find what it was so that someone else could be charged for it.

'And where have *you* been?' she said, trying to sound severe.

'Flying,' he said. 'I finished with my workspace for today . . .' He sighed a little, vanished his suit. 'It will take a while to get it the way I want it.'

'You didn't take it out in the real game, did you?'

She looked at him narrowly. 'Well,' he said. 'Yes.'

'Oh, come on, Laurent,' she said. 'I promised I would make sure you didn't overdo it. And what if the Archon had come along with one of his fleets?'

'But the Archon was blown up. In the Big Bang.'

Maj blew out an annoyed breath. 'You know they'll just clone him from the bits and pieces,' she said. 'In fact there are probably clones sitting around on Darkworld right now waiting to be uncanned and reprogrammed. He could have turned up the next day!'

'But he did not. And besides, you said it would have

been tactically unwise.' He grinned at her.

'Space lawyer,' Maj said. 'Come on, lose the suit. I hear that Mom is going to make her famous impaled lamb chops with garlic stuck all through them.'

Laurent concentrated and vanished the suit. 'What does it mean,' he said as they walked back to the door to Maj's space, 'when you try to make something in the workspace, and it fails?'

'It's just incomplete visualization,' Maj said. 'All kinds of reasons for that. In your case, you're still getting used to the hardware-software interface . . . failures are common.' She looked around her at the soft evening light coming through the high windows in her own workspace as they stepped through the door. 'You should have seen how long it took me to get this right. The lighting, the synchronization to local time. The sounds, the smells . . .' She looked at the floor with amusement. 'And the carpet kept changing color. It drove me crazy until I found out why it did that. I'd stolen the "template" from a carpet company ad online . . . and every time they changed the ad, the rug changed too . . .'

'But there is no rug here.'

'No, I got rid of it.' She smiled a rather embarrassed smile. 'See, I didn't find out what I was doing wrong until much later. I vanished the carpet and put in hardwood flooring . . . and *then* found out. But look, Laurent, really, your dad said that he didn't want you to spend *too* much time Netside, and I—'

The door on the other side of the workspace opened, and a tall, gangly young man wearing fluorescent floppy clothes and a marked resemblance to Maj's father looked in. 'Maj, is your friend – oh, here he is. Hi there.'

'Laurent, this is the famous Rick you keep hearing about,' Maj said. 'The phantom stranger.'

'When I'm home all the time she complains,' Rick said, coming over to shake Laurent's hand. 'When I'm not home all the time, she complains. Let me give you advice – don't have any sisters.'

'Oh, I don't know,' Laurent said, a little shyly, as they made their way back to the door. 'Yours seem all right.'

'Huh,' said Rick, an all-purpose sound of skepticism, and embarked on a list of Maj's weak points, all spurious as far as Laurent could tell, while Maj followed her brother through the door into his own workspace and made scathing comments about his dress sense. Laurent smiled a little as he followed them through the space, which resembled nothing else so much as a huge warehouse piled up with wildly assorted objects of all kinds. 'Welcome to Icon World,' Maj said to Laurent. 'My brother is a little object-oriented, as you can see. Rick, was there a *reason* for this intrusion, or were you just practicing being a nuisance?'

'Oh, I heard you doing the "behaviour Police" act and thought I'd come see what it looks like when you do it to *other* people . . . This door shuts your implant off,' Rick said to Laurent while stepping over the sill of another doorway which was standing, incongruously, in the middle of the huge warehouse space. 'I understand that your presence is being requested in what we laughably refer to as the Real World.'

A moment later, Laurent found himself sitting in the implant chair in the Greens' den, and the sound of someone running down the hall made him stand up. A few seconds later the Muffin came charging in and grabbed him around the legs. 'I have to read to you now,' she announced, breathless.

'That depends. When is dinner?' Laurent said.

'Half an hour,' said Maj, putting her head in through

the doorway. 'Muffin, no dinosaurs now. You've exceeded your Net time for today. And so have *you*,' she said, wagging a finger at Laurent, 'so behave.'

'We will be good,' Laurent said, with a rather helpless smile as the Muffin grabbed his hand and dragged him out of the den and toward her room. Maj smiled at him and went off; and Laurent, following the Muffin, reflected that though the family he preferred the most was his own, there were others which could, very temporarily, make an acceptable distraction.

He found his hands shaking just a little, a fine muscle tremor, as he sat down on the Muffin's bed and watched her start rooting through her bookshelves. *The jetlag is finally catching up with me,* he thought. *Or maybe it's just nerves. Why am I spending time scaring myself? Things are happening as fast as they can. And Popi is smart . . . smarter than they are. He'll be here soon enough, and if I'm wrecked with worrying, he won't be happy.*

Laurent let out a long breath and watched the Muffin settle down on the floor and open the book . . .

The Quality House Suite in Alexandria was the same as all the other hotels in the chain, or so the Major heard one businessman telling another over drinks in the hotel's downstairs bar. Herself, she could not understand what his problem was. There was nothing wrong with one hotel being like another. The same kind of service everywhere, what was wrong with that? These people were too individualistic for their own good.

She tried to put the locals' quirks out of her mind, though it was hard, stuck here among the millions of them, trapped in all this offensive opulence and conspicuous consumption. This whole country was vulgar, a vast expanse of expenditure for its own sake, money spent just to prove it was there in the first place. Other countries would have used these resources more wisely . . . if they had had them, and if this country had not spent so much time and spite making sure that other countries did *not*.

Well, the Major thought, sipping her mineral water as she sat alone at the little table in the hotel lounge and made shorthand notes on a pad, *they will soon see the tables turned, for a change. Once this recovery operation is over and the results start to be developed, our balance of payments should show a great improvement . . . and the countries around us which have been so busily shoring up their connections to the western democracies will start wondering whether they should have looked closer to home for financial aid. Not that they will get any from us . . . not now. They have shown all too clearly where their loyalties lie.*

But that was in the future. Right now the Major was busy reviewing what had been done since she arrived, making sure everything was sorted out. It was no small matter to arrange the theft of an ambulance, but she was working on it. Money talked, even to the local organized crime groups, and she thought she would shortly have all the necessary resources in place. She already had what little weaponry she needed – in this country there was never any problem with that, no matter what the government said. Its own people, unable or unwilling to discriminate between their condition now and that of three hundred years ago, had it hamstrung *there*. In any case, it would not be firepower that would make the difference to this operation, but speed, surprise, and the amount of traffic between here and the Embassy. Two out of three of those elements, the Major could control. They would be more than enough.

She folded up her pad and put it away in her sidepack, and sipped at her mineral water again. Things were now progressing nicely. Her source back home had informed her via coded message to her pager that the first 'burst' signal had been sent – the microps were awake and accepting new programming, and would also relay directional information the next time they boy was in the Net. Now the clock was running. Within about twenty-four hours, there would be a call for an ambulance . . . and she would be ready with its 'crew' to take the poor sick boy someplace where he would be "properly" cared for.

Something bleeped softly behind the concierge's desk, and he looked up. 'Mrs Lejeune?' he called. 'Your car is here.'

'Thank you,' the Major said. She finished her mineral water, then walked out the front to where the rental car had just settled into the pickup pad.

She slid in behind the driver's seat, lined up her implant with the car's Net access, and let it confirm her identity and credit information – all very routine stuff, which (having been planted here long since by her own service) confirmed that she was Mrs Alice Lejeune of Baton Rouge, owner of a small printing company. Anyone at Avis whose eye happened to fall on her rental details would think she was probably up here on business, just as the people at the hotel had.

She knew exactly where she was going, for she had memorized the maps before ever passing her own country's borders. The Major drove sedately for some miles, idly noting the scenery. This whole area had become relentlessly suburban over the years, affluent, smug. Well, there was at least one family here which would have its

177

smugness ruffled somewhat in the next twenty-four or thirty-six hours.

She hung a right out of the main north-south artery, letting the car drive on auto for the moment while she activated the small videocamera she had brought with her, using it to look around and take careful note of what cars were parked in this area. One of her assistants would be making another pass later, in another locally-registered car, to compare those images with these. She was fairly sure that Professor Green would have called for some kind of external surveillance by now. But over the next twelve hours the Major and the operatives who had been onsite until now would get a complete record of which vehicles were the same, which ones changed . . . which were registered to genuine locals, and which belonged to people trying not to look like they were keeping an eye on the Greens' house.

The Major looked down as the car turned right and proceeded along the small quiet suburban street . . . and there it was. A longish house, looking as if it had been built in stages. A front door with steps leading down to the standard suburban front walk through the standard suburban lawn. A back door leading out into a large fenced garden with a child's playset. A garage, not connected to the house, and a driveway in front of it, with the family car sitting on it at the moment. Lights on in several rooms and – as she pulled down her 'sunglasses' and looked through them – one, two, three, four, five, six blurred heat-shapes in the dining room, with other shapes over to one side; the oven, the refrigerator, the microwave.

Family dinner. How charming.

In her mind she made note of the entrance and exit routes – distances, obstacles – and smiled slightly. Shortly the Greens' suburban bliss would receive a wakeup call. Well, they would have brought it on themselves. And Professor Green in particular would be taught a sharp lesson in not interfering in other countries' affairs. At the national level there was no hope that any notice would be taken . . . but at the personal level, she imagined there would. The message would be plain enough. *This could have been* your *children. Back off, become wiser . . . or next time, it* might *be.*

The car continued on by. The Major sat back, looking at the last dregs of the broad sullen sunset, and smiling slightly at the prospect of action. *Tomorrow, about this time, or a little later.*

Poor little Laurent . . . I'm sure you've had a nice holiday. But now it's time to go home.

The evening tapered off into one of those informal we're-all-here-at-once-isn't-it-amazing? family evenings which were Maj's favorite kind, rather than the more structured 'family nights' which her father insisted on once a week, usually on Thursdays unless something more important got in the way. Dinner was spectacular, and the family breathed garlic happily at one another all evening – no one moved from the table for a long time, everyone seeming content to just sit around talking about life, the news, the various levels of school the family had to deal with, and so on. Laurent was plainly enjoying himself, but to Maj's surprise, he was the first one to excuse himself and get up. 'I think the jetlag is finally getting to me,' he said.

Maj's father looked at him with some concern. 'Do you feel all right? You look a little pale, actually.'

'Just a headache,' Laurent said.

'Poor dear. Maj, show him where the asprothingies are,' her mother said.

'Sure, come on . . .' Maj took him down to the bathroom, thumbprinted the medicine cabinet open, and rummaged around for the soluble aspirin that one of her father's colleagues in England sent over once every few months. 'This stuff is great . . . it has no taste at all. Two in water every four hours.' She reached up for a glass and half filled it with water, dropped the tablets in.

'Thanks,' Laurent said.

She looked at him thoughtfully. It wasn't just the bathroom light – he really did look pale. 'I wonder if you might have picked up a flu bug or something on the way in,' she said. 'All those people in the airport, after all . . . a new country, lots of new strains of germs . . .'

'I don't know,' Laurent said. 'But I'm tired, all of a sudden. I wasn't tired before, not like this.'

'Huh. Well, look, why not turn in early?'

'Turn in?'

'Sorry . . . idiom. Go to bed.'

'I might,' he said, and sagged against the doorsill a little, watching the tablets fizz themselves away.

'Did this just hit you?' Maj said.

'Yes. Or maybe not. I felt shivery while I was . . . when I was inside *Cluster Rangers*. It wasn't anything, I didn't pay any attention to it.' He shrugged now. 'You are probably right . . . it is probably just the flu.'

'I don't know,' Maj said. 'I've been online often enough when I was sick, and that's just where you *don't* feel it – the interface cuts your "normal" bodily reactions out of the loop. You might have noticed,' Maj added with some amusement, 'the first time you'd been there for a couple of hours and then found out real suddenly that you needed to visit the bathroom . . .'

He laughed at that, looking wry. 'Yes.'

'I learned real early to lay off the fluids before simming,' Maj said. 'Still, it's a little weird . . . Well, look, get some rest.'

The liquid in the glass finished its fizzing. Laurent picked it up, drank it down. 'There is no taste,' he said.

'Believe me,' Maj said, 'I prefer that to my brother's method. He chews up aspirin tablets whole. Says the taste doesn't bother him.' She shuddered.

So did Laurent. '*That* felt like a chill,' he said mournfully. 'The flu, then. What a nuisance.'

'We've got some stuff in here that's good for that,' Maj said. 'One of the new multiplex antivirals. Wait a few hours to see if it really is the flu . . . then take one of these.' She reached into the cabinet again, showed him the box. 'Same deal – two in a glass of water, then go lie down . . . because it'll knock you on your butt.'

Laurent smiled a little wanly. 'Idiom,' Maj said.

'But I understood that one.'

'Go on,' Maj said, 'go crash out. You've been through enough lately that you shouldn't be surprised if it catches up with you.'

He headed off for the guest room. Maj made her way back into the kitchen, where her mother was talking the Muffin into getting ready to go to bed, and her father was leaning back in his chair discussing curling with her brother. 'Is he okay?' her dad said as Maj sat back down.

'He thinks he might be flu-ish,' Maj said. 'He's had a couple of chills.'

'Could be,' her mother said, and sighed. 'That airport is always full of germs from exotic parts of the world, looking for new people to bite. Did you show him where the virus stuff was?'

'Yeah,' Maj said. 'He'll know better than any of us if he needs it.'

'All right,' her mother said. 'I just don't like to think of him being sick here alone. It's busy the next couple of nights. You have that alumni thing again—'

'I can cancel if I have to,' Maj's father said. 'Any excuse.'

'That's not what you said last night,' her mother said. 'You said it was important. And I have that consultant's meeting with the Net-dorks at PsiCor – heaven only knows how late *that's* going to run . . . they kept me till ten last time. And you're off sliding stones as usual,' she said to Rick.

'Mom, don't sweat it, I'll be here,' Maj said. 'I'm flying with some of the Group tomorrow night. We were going to take Niko with us, but one way or another, I'll be on site. It's just the flu, anyway.'

'Yes, but he's in a strange place . . .'

'Mom,' Maj said, 'he doesn't need his diaper changed, either. No need to do the Great Earth Mother thing.' She grinned a little. 'You just go play kick-the-client as scheduled. Everything will be fine.'

'Yes, of course,' her mother said, and got up. 'Come on, Miss Muffin, let's get you in the restraints for the night.' She picked up the giggling, wriggling Muffin and carried her down the hall, shushing her as they went.

'He's a nice kid,' Rick said. 'Has he shown any interest in sports?'

'You mean in sliding rocks around on ice?' Maj said with good-natured scorn. 'He's shown much better sense than that. I think we're going to make a simmer out of him.'

'A complete waste,' her brother said, getting up and

stretching. 'Oh well.' He got up and started picking up dishes.

Maj looked at her dad. 'You could always use the excuse,' she said.

'No, your mom's right,' he said. 'Duty before pleasure. Unfortunately.' He got up and started collecting silverware, and Maj rose to help him clear things away, it being the rule in the Green household that The Cook Doesn't Clean But Everyone Else Does.

Her brother chuckled. 'Smart kid,' he said, 'absenting himself before the cleaning frenzy was due to begin. He'll go far.'

'He didn't know,' Maj said. 'And I don't think he would have avoided it, frankly . . .' All the same, she found herself fretting in a mode similar to the one in which she had spent much of the day at school.

It's just the flu. He'll be fine.

But if I'm so sure, then why am I twitching like this?

In the small dark room, six thousand miles away, a man sat in the predawn darkness listening to his little radio through his earphone. At the end of each day's first news broadcast, and after the day's last one at six, there was always a reading of personal announcements which people had phoned or linked in to the national broadcaster – sometimes notices for people travelling in the country, sometimes mundane announcements like details about sales or a change in the time of a local country market, news about police roadblocks (at least, the ones they wanted you to know about) or information about where the roads were being worked on. Armin listened to each of these broadcasts every day, waiting for the one that would tell him that his unknown friends were ready to help him leave the cellar, and the country, for the last time. Now he sat waiting, tense as always, getting more impatient all the time as announcement after announcement was read, and none of them were for him.

'. . . the A41 national road at Soara, we regret to inform travelers that this road will be closed for the next two weeks due to bridge repairs on the route. Travelers are advised to use the A16 road through Elmila instead . . .Leoru Town Market will start at eight fifteen next Saturday morning rather than at nine fifteen as previously scheduled . . .To Bela Urnim, presently traveling to Timisoara on business—'

The breath went into him in a gasp, got stuck there.

'—we have received your message of the eighteenth and understand it.'

Armin sat up convulsively against the wall, feeling his hands go cold with fear all in an instant. That was one of the code phrases in the book given him by the organization that had been helping him, the book which he had memorized. This one phrase had stuck particularly in his mind even before everything was committed to memory, because he had often wondered in what circumstances it might be used. And now he knew.

It meant, *All is betrayed.*

Armin began to shake.

'Your shipment has been collected at its destination by Customs and the information which you designated before leaving is being used to process it,' the uncomprehending voice reading the announcement went on. 'The processing of perishable materials will be complete in twenty-four hours. You have that long to contact us regarding your desires regarding further handling. Otherwise the contents of the shipment will be disposed of. This is a message for

Gelei Vanni, travelling from Organte to—'

He pulled the earphone out of his ear, turned the radio off, dropped it on the dirty floor.

They have him.

He covered his face in his hands. *I thought he was safe. I was a fool. They've found a way to get at him.*

And they've activated the microps . . .

He rubbed his eyes, trying desperately to get hold of himself, for now he had to think, *think*. One of his associates had broken – no telling which. Sasha, or Donae, possibly. They would have known the machine codes for the microps which Laurent was carrying – there was a set of master codes which all the little creatures had been built to answer to in case of the need for an emergency shutdown. Now the police had those. And they had used them in the most effective manner possible, from their point of view.

His friends were all betrayed – they could not help him now. And the meaning of the message was clear enough. Come out and give yourself up, and we will spare your son's life. Keep hiding, and . . .

Armin stopped rubbing his eyes. All too clearly in memory he could see the slides from the brains of the poor rats who had suffered from the 'mistake', the ones in whom the microps had run wild for only half a day. That was happening right now, inside his son. It would take longer . . . but not much longer. They would now be migrating to his spinal column to make their way up through the cerebrospinal fluid into the brain. Once there, they would start pulling the myofibrils apart, chewing away at the myelin that coated and interconnected the brain cells. In eighteen hours, his son would be seriously ill. In twenty-four, he would be on his way to being a vegetable.

All he had to do now, to stop it, was give himself up.

And after that he would be made to recreate his work – especially, he knew, the dark side of it. If he did not, they would threaten Laurent again. Or they would simply kill them both, and hand his work over to someone else to continue. For they had Laurent – and dead or alive, they would be able to get enough information from whichever of his associates had cracked to get the microps out again. After that they would not care what happened to him.

Armin sat there for what seemed an eternity, in the darkness, frozen and trying to think what to do. It was, in reality, about five minutes. *There's no point in fighting any longer*, he told himself. *They have him. It's all over now. If you're going to save him, you must act quickly.*

Yet there was still another part of him, stubborn, sullen, angry, which was unwilling to give up while he was still breathing. There was one last chance. Very slim, not likely to do any good . . . but he had to try it. For Laurent's sake, as much as for his own.

Armin sighed, reached into the deep pocket in his trousers, and came up with the cell phone.

He had purposely not used the cell phone at all for the last few days, had not even turned it on, because its signal could be all too easily targeted . . . assuming he was in a location where it would even work. But he had been given a number to call if things went badly wrong, a last-resort number which he could call only once.

This seemed like the time to use it.

Armin thumbed the button to turn it on, and waited.

Waited. Breathless.

Then, after about ten seconds, a single bar of light appeared above the little 'antenna' symbol. The phone was close enough to an antenna to successfully dial out.

He hurriedly touched in the quick-dial code and put the phone to his ear.

It rang.

It rang for at least thirty seconds, and Armin hung on, beginning to shake. It was not safe to have the phone active even this long and he didn't dare activate it twice.

Someone picked up the phone. 'Yes,' said the voice, in English.

He told them who he was, and where he was, all in a quick burst of words; and he told them why he was calling.

'We know,' said the voice on the other end.

'Help me,' was all he could say. 'My son . . .' And he ran out of breath.

'We'll try,' said the voice. 'No guarantees.'

'I know. Thank you.'

'Don't thank us yet,' said the voice, and hung up.

He stared at the now-mute chunk of plastic and put it back in his pocket, and then breathed out and put his head down on his knees. It was all he could do.

It was all he had time to do . . . for, in the next breath, he heard them outside, hammering at the old painted-over door with something heavy. He heard the ancient rusty padlock break.

And then with a screech, and another screech, the old doors were levered open, and the light of dawn came flooding in, blinding him. His eyes watered, so that he could barely make out the uniformed shape that came down the stairs, silhouetted against the light. He did not need to see details. He knew who put hands under his arms, who helped him up and walked him, staggering slightly, up the stairs.

It was Death.

Eight

Maj did not sleep well that night, and she was up unusually early, even for her. What surprised her somewhat, when she pulled on jeans and a T-shirt and meandered into the kitchen for her first cup of tea, was finding her father there before her. He wouldn't normally have been up for another half-hour or so – but here he was, nursing a cup of coffee, cold from the look of it, and wearing a haggard expression.

'Daddy?' she said, starting to go over to the kettle . . . and then stopping. There was only one thing she could think of which would make him look so bleak. 'Did you hear anything?'

'He nodded. He looked down the hall first to see who might be there, and then said softly, 'I got a call from James Winters about fifteen minutes ago. Their information-service people who listen to the media over there picked up an announcement on the morning news. They've arrested Armin Darenko.'

'Oh no,' Maj said, and forgot about the kettle, and went to sit down at the table – her legs felt weak under her all of a sudden. 'Oh, no, it's not fair—'

'I don't know that fairness comes into it,' her dad said, looking into the coffee, 'but I feel terrible.'

'You're not alone,' Maj said. She gulped. 'What happens now?'

He shook his head. 'I don't know. James didn't seem to think there was a lot of chance of getting him away from them again. The country is so isolated and so tightly sealed . . . and just so paranoid . . . that new people can't easily blend in. Operatives from *any* friendly force are very thin on the ground.'

'Will they—' Maj gulped again. It was odd how it was suddenly hard to think. 'They're going to try to do something to Laurent now, aren't they?'

'They may have it in mind,' her father said, 'but I doubt they'll get far. The house is being watched twenty-four hours a day, James tells me. Net Force, and others.'

Somehow Maj did not feel particularly relieved. It had seemed to her that there had been rather more cars than usual parked around here the last couple of days. She was almost able to be slightly pleased with herself for having noticed that, even subliminally. Not that there had been people in the cars, either . . . but that did not mean that they could not have been wired for eighteen different kinds of surveillance.

She sat looking at the table for a moment, and at her hands, folded in front of her, and then looked up again at her father, who was staring unseeing at his coffee cup.

'Daddy,' she said, very slowly, 'are you sure they *haven't* found a way to do something to Laurent?'

Her father looked at her blankly.

'Is he still sick?'

'Uh, yes,' her father said. 'I looked in to see if he wanted to go running . . . he said no, and turned over. He doesn't look very well. And frankly, I don't feel much like running myself, now.'

'Fine . . . but don't you think it's kind of a coincidence that this should have happened to him right *now?*'

Her father looked at her a little strangely. 'Maj, you wouldn't normally strike me as the conspiracy-theory type. There's no evidence to support such a conclusion.'

'I know, but—' Maj shook her head. 'Dad, he said he started to feel funny while he was online.'

Her father shook his head too. 'Good thing there's no such thing as a genuine "Net virus",' he said. 'I'd hate to think what could happen if there was one. But whatever may be the matter with him, you can't catch diseases on the Net.'

'That's certainly what they tell us,' Maj said.

'By the way,' her father said, 'James tells me that apparently someone tried to get into Laurent's accounts, the other night.'

Maj was horrified. 'Did they?'

'Of course not. Those accounts are apparently on Net Force's own servers, and they've got firewalls like the Great Wall of China. God Himself would have to call their sysop and ask her for a password.' He sighed. 'All the same, I don't like it. Leaving aside the matter of his father's capture, they're snooping around Laurent pretty actively . . . and Laurent is here.'

'This extra security, this surveillance . . . do you think it's enough?'

'I think maybe the less said about that, the better,' her father said softly. 'But I'm told we're safe, honey.'

'It's not us I'm worried about,' said Maj. 'It's Laurent.'

The look her father gave her was just slightly humorous, the first normal-looking expression he had produced in this conversation. 'Fortunately,' he said, 'I know what you meant by that. But my concerns are elsewhere, too. Your mother. You and Rick. The Muffin.'

Maj swallowed. The thought of someone from a hostile country's intelligence services coming here to try to get Laurent, and possibly hurting the Muffin instead – it was too horrifying to think about . . .

'And I always knew that this might happen,' her dad said. 'So we just need to keep our eyes open, all of us. Except the Muf, whose composure I'm not going to disturb with all of this, for reasons you'll understand. A six-year-old has enough to do, coping with the world we're living in nowadays, without thinking that the bad people might actually come to her house and try to kidnap someone she reads to.'

He sighed. 'As for Laurent, I'm not sure this is exactly the best time to break this news to him, either.'

Maj flushed hot suddenly. 'Daddy,' she said, 'he's not a child.'

'Uh, excuse me, oh ancient of days . . . but he *is* a child.'

'You know what I mean! You were the first one to suggest that he was a little "older" in the brain than usual. You can't keep this from him. Someone's going to have to tell him eventually!'

Her father rubbed his face. 'Yes,' he said. 'I agree with you. But not right this minute, all right?' He looked up at her then. 'Besides . . . there's always the possibility that something may happen.'

' "Something"?' She looked at him.

He stood up, turned away from her. 'Don't ask me for details,' he said. 'I can't give them to you. But in the meantime, let's just sit on this piece of information for a day or so, and hope that it changes.'

He dumped the cold coffee in the sink. 'Mom will be here today,' he said. 'You'll be back before she and I have to go out again. Just keep an eye on things, and don't get panicky, all right?'

'I won't panic,' she said. 'I don't usually.'

'I know you don't,' her father said, and kissed her on the top of her head in passing; then went on down to the bedroom to get dressed.

Maj sat there for a good while, with her chin propped on her enlaced fingers, and cursed the unfairness of the world. Then she too got up and got dressed to go to school.

The day was sheer hell. Maj could not keep her mind on anything. Her shattered concentration cost her many points on a math test for which she had had great hopes, having studied for the damn thing for a good chunk of the last week – but Venn diagrams seemed strangely useless to her today. And it was Laurent's father, more than anything else, whose case was on her mind. Laurent might be sick, but he was safe. His father was now in some little bare room with a light trained on his face by the bad guys – the 'bad room' from all those old movies . . . and there was nothing that could be done about it. Think how you would feel if *your* father were in that room, Maj thought. *Dad's right. It's too awful. Let Laurent wait a while to find out . . . until he feels better, anyway.*

But *she* knew . . . and she was not going to feel any better. It was all profoundly depressing. Maj dragged herself from class to class all day, causing a couple of her teachers to ask her what the matter was. She used the excuse that it was 'something physiological,' which was vague enough to be true, since it was someone else's physiology on her mind, but also served to make them stop asking her questions. When the last bell went, she tore out of the place and headed for the bus home. It was delayed, which drove her wild, but she waited for it, rode it the whole way, and then got off and forced herself not to run the last couple of blocks . . . because she was afraid of who might be watching.

It was five o'clock when she walked in the door. Her Mom met her; she was in the process of getting ready to go out to her consultants' meeting.

'Laurent's still under the weather. It could very well be flu,' her mother said, putting a loose-leaf full of printouts into her carrybag. 'I gave him some more aspirin, and the antiviral. The fever came down a little. But he doesn't have much appetite. It's a good thing he's not showing any sensitivity to light, or I'd be a lot more worried.'

That made Maj feel a little better. 'Has Daddy been back yet?' Maj said.

'Been and gone,' her Mom said, 'just to pick up his suit. He'll be back first, I bet.' It was a grumble.

'I don't know, Mom . . .' Maj smiled a little.

'I gave the Muffin a little early dinner,' her mother said, picking up the big shoulder bag full of printouts and loose-leaf notebooks, and her portable Net machine with her consultancy-business files in it. 'Let's see . . .' She stopped in the front doorway to see if she needed anything else. 'Nope, all together. These people are living in the information age, for pity's sake, I don't see why they insist on making me come out to their pestilent meetings when we could all sit comfortably in our *homes* and have them.'

'It's a power trip,' Maj said. 'They're all relics . . . they'll retire soon, I bet.'

'From your mouth to the Great Programmer's ear,' Maj's mother said. She kissed her daughter, and said, 'Lock up, now.' She glanced down the hall, toward Laurent's room.

'I will,' Maj said.

Her mom pushed the door open. 'Oh, and I forgot, there's a letter from Auntie Elenya there for you . . .'

'A letter? Wow,' Maj said, as her mother pulled the door shut. 'See you, Mom . . .'

The car revved up outside, whirred away. Maj threw the solenoid bolt on the front door and turned to the little table where the paper mail sat when it had come in. Sure enough, there was an airmail envelope – Maj picked it up, saw her name at the top of the typed address.

'How about that,' she said. The letter was postmarked WIEN – that was where they lived, she and Maj's uncle, the Mad Cartographer. She tore it open, unfolded the thin airmail paper with pleasure. It was unusual to get paper mail from the relatives any more, now that they were all online. Mostly it came in the form of postcards, they—

'Dear Madeline,' the first sheet said in English. 'I have sent this note to you for my son. It seemed more likely to reach you without interference—'

Maj nearly dropped it – then took a breath, and started to fold it up again – then stopped herself and opened it once more. *It was addressed to me, after all. He would have realized I would probably read at least some of it—*

'I want to thank you and your family for agreeing to make him welcome. There is, however, some information which you and he will need to know now, since it may take me a short time before I am able to follow him—'

Maj read the letter, and felt her hands starting to shake. She turned the page over, read the other side.

Then she went straight down the hall to Laurent's room, and knocked. 'Nggh?' he said.

She opened the door and put her head in. 'I'm sorry to bother you,' she said, 'but you had better see this. And then we're going to have to decide what to do . . .'

★ ★ ★

About ten minutes later Laurent was still sitting on the edge of the bed, looking profoundly uncomfortable . . . and not just because of his illness. Sluggish as he was, Laurent had started to read the letter for the third time, and then had stopped himself and laid it aside.

'They are inside me,' he said. He shook his head. 'The only ones left from all his work. That last cup of tea . . .'

'Could be,' Maj said.

Laurent looked at her, somewhat unnerved. 'Still,' he said. 'My father made them. They would never hurt me.'

'If they were still running your father's programming,' Maj said, very softly, 'no. I *do* understand, now, why you looked so good, the first couple of days. The little monsters have been running around inside you, pulling the lactic acid molecules apart, keeping you healthy . . .'

'They do not seem to be doing that any more,' he said. 'Maybe they, too, are jetlagged?'

'What do you think the odds of *that* are?' Maj said. She swallowed. 'Laurent . . . there's one other piece of news that wasn't in the letter.'

He looked at her, eyes wide at her tone of voice.

She told him about the arrest.

It was a good few moments before he spoke again. 'Then they have been interrogating all the people he worked with,' Laurent said. 'Anything they knew, the internal police now know. Or soon will.'

'Including,' Maj said, 'I very strongly suspect, how to reprogram your little friends the microps. Laurent . . . I don't think they're your friends any more. I would bet you serious money that the internal police or whatever were waiting for you to go online. And when you did – they reprogrammed them . . . and then told your father that if

196

he didn't come out from where he was hiding, they'd leave them running.'

Laurent looked stricken. Maj herself was fighting with a huge load of guilt which she would otherwise have wallowed in for a good while. *Dad told me, Laurent's dad told him, to keep him off the Net – why didn't we take him seriously! Or seriously enough!* But there was no time to waste on self-recrimination right now. They were going to have to do something.

'I think you are right,' he said. 'That chill last night . . .'

'Yes. And now the problem is, where do we go from here? Because the next thing they'll do, I bet, is try to get their hands on you. The prototypes, the only ones there are, are swimming around inside you . . . and no one else knows about it yet. Though they will in about five minutes – because once Net Force and the people over here know, not all Cluj's horses and all Cluj's men are going to be able to touch you.'

Laurent still had a fairly shocked look. 'We need to get moving,' Maj said, 'because Mom's gone now, and Dad won't be back, and I bet you money they'll decide that this is a great time to make a move, while there's no one home but the kids.'

'The kids—' He looked even more shocked. 'The Muffin is here . . .'

That had been on Maj's mind, too.

'I would not want anything to happen to the Muffin. She is special.'

'No argument there.' Maj said.

'Even if she does make me sit with her while she reads to dinosaurs with bad breath.'

That made Maj burst out laughing. She much needed a laugh, for she was starting to shake inside. 'Look,' she said.

'None of this is your fault. But we've got to move.'

'And do what?' Laurent said, sounding as helpless as Maj felt. 'They are inside me. I do not know anything about them – not the important part, anyway, not anything about the codes that would stop them. I am sure that only my father and the government have those . . . and the government will not issue them unless—' He broke off.

For the first time, Maj saw his face start to crumple toward tears. But he held them off. 'I do not want to be a weapon,' he muttered. 'But that is what they will use me for. That is what I am, Maj! They are using me for that right now. I will not let them use me that way! It would be better if I was—'

'Don't say it,' Maj said. 'It's a lot too soon to start making decisions like that.' All the same, she was not going to *there-there* him or waste her time with other arguments. There was a toughness about this kid that made Maj suspect he would do something that desperate if he felt there was need . . . because he really did love his dad that much. 'Besides,' she said, 'they may not know what they're dealing with here.'

'Which is what?'

'Which is us,' she said. 'We're plenty . . . so let's move first. Get into your sweats, get into the den, get online.'

'Is that a good idea?' he said. 'I am really sick. Things are starting to hurt, Maj . . .'

The thought immediately went through her mind – call an ambulance, get him to the hospital. She hesitated—

—then rejected it. The hospital would not be able to do anything. To get Laurent well, these little monsters needed to be deactivated. Then they needed to be removed. The hospital emergency room would be equipped for neither. *Better to keep him safe here*, Maj thought *and not let him out of my sight until someone from Net Force shows up.*

And until then . . . there has to be a way to fight them.
. . . But boy, this sure doesn't match the nice evening we had
planned. A peaceful evening with a few of the Group, out in the
depths of—

And the idea came to her. It was not complete, but Maj
had a few minutes for that yet. *Broad strokes first,* she
thought, *then fill in the detail—* 'Go on,' she said to
Laurent. 'Dress, get moving, we don't have a lot of time!'

He got up and started rummaging around for his sweats.
Maj ran for the machine in her Mom's office, threw herself
into the chair, lined up the implant, flung herself into her
workspace. 'Red alert,' she said to the workspace, and the
intervention lighting in the big room came on all around
her. It was atmosphere, nothing more, but it made her feel
better. 'Panic button call, James Winters!'

There was an intolerably long pause. 'The party you are
calling is not available,' the system said. 'Please leave a
message.'

'Where is he?!' Maj yelled.

'That information is private. If you have clearance of
level 8 or better, please state your clearance number.'

'Never mind that.' She gulped. 'Panic button call, Jay
Gridley!'

'The party you are calling is not available. Please leave a
message.'

'Tell him to call Maj Green immediately. This is an
emergency. End call,' Maj said. She took a long breath,
and tried to calm herself and sort out the sequence for
what she was going to have to do.

Call Dad, scream for help. Good, but anyone could tap
into a cell phone call these days, and she had no desire at
all to advertise to Laurent's dad's enemies that she was

onto them. Nonetheless, she had to tell her dad about this and get him to drop what he was doing and come help. *Leave a message for Winters, let him know what you need and what you're going to do.* There must be someone's desk that his urgent-tagged messages land on. *Then yell for other help. Someone who can help me defend Laurent while the high-powered stuff is coming.*

In the end, she called her dad's phone. As she was afraid, it was turned off. She left a message tagged MOST URGENT on it, telling him to come straight home. Then she called James Winters' code again, got the same message, and this time left a detailed message a minute and a half long, tagged UTMOST URGENCY.

She stopped, then, took a breath. 'Group of Seven call,' Maj said. 'Del.'

'Working,' the machine said. A moment later, there he was, sitting out in his back yard.

'You're early,' Del said.

'Better than being late,' Maj said, somewhat grimly. 'This is a New Force Explorer problem, Del. Can you suit up and meet me in my space? Right now.'

He clambered out of the lawn lounge he was lying in. 'And do me a favor,' Maj said. 'Get Robin, too. I'm a little pressed for time here.'

'This isn't about the game?'

'Oh, it is,' she said, 'but the stakes have been raised a little. We're talking life and death here. The real thing, not the virtual type.'

Del stared at her. 'Three minutes,' he said.

She broke out of virtuality, met Laurent in the hall. 'Okay,' she said, 'the ball's rolling. I'm going to shut the house up. And if I have to, I'll call the cops as well. I have no idea what they'll make of it, but it'll sure annoy anyone from your government who shows up thinking they're going to take you for a ride in the next little while.'

'But how can this matter? If the microps—'

'We can't stop them,' she said. 'But maybe we can fight them. Look, Laurent, why are you arguing with me? If you get into the machine, it'll at least cut your sensoria out of the loop, and you won't feel sick.' *Until you go unconscious. And how long will that be? Oh, God—!*

'Fight them? With what?' he said, staggering a little.

'The power of geekery,' she said, 'and the power of good. Better hope that's enough. Get in there and get online!'

She put him in the implant chair in her dad's den, pulling down the blinds and drawing the drapes. 'I don't want you to panic,' Maj said, 'but I'm going to lock you in, okay? If they try anything—'

'All right,' he said.

'Meet me in my workspace as soon as you get in. Get suited up. We're going flying.'

She went around the house as calmly as she could, making sure all the windows were locked, all the doors shut, and pulling blinds and curtains closed everywhere. In her room the Muffin was sitting reading, for once. As Maj put her head in, the Muffin lifted a finger to her lips and said, '*SSSSH*. Laurent's sick.'

'I know he is, honey,' Maj said. 'I want you to come and be in mommy's office with me.'

'Okay. Are you going online?'

'Yes, sweetie.'

'Okay.'

Maj escorted the little one into her mom's office and made her comfortable on an old beanbag chair in the corner, which immediately began, in its traditional manner, leaking its little polystyrene 'beans.'

201

'Dumb thing,' Maj muttered, shut the blinds and drew the curtains in the office, and then went out to make the rest of the house secure, finishing by setting the alarm system. It would not stop anyone who was really intent on getting in . . . but it would slow them down, and time might start mattering a whole lot shortly. And it would automatically alert the local police if something disturbed the signal in any way.

She stood still there in the kitchen for a moment, and thought. Nothing more she could do about the physical security now. That was going to have to be the waiting part of this game. If she called the police now, she would only get in trouble for wasting their time. Who would believe her if she told them what was going on here? The local branch police station was only about five minutes away – that was close enough . . . she hoped. She had a panic button call set up in her workspace with their name on it, too, as well as the auto-alert wired into the alarm system. She could shout for help any time she needed it.

Nothing to do now but get the battle organized. The main trouble was the medical expertise. If it had been the insides of a horse Maj had been dealing with, it would have been another story entirely. But you could not use veterinary science on people. The biology didn't universally apply to humans. Not when it was something this delicate. *Who do I know? Who do I—?*

Charlie! Charlie Davis.

If he was around. *Oh, please, let him be around . . .*

She dove into her Mom's office again, locked the door. The Muffin was oblivious, still deep in the copy of *Rewards and Fairies. Thank you, Rudyard,* Maj thought, *I owe you one . . .* She lined up the implant, plunged into her workspace again. There stood Laurent, in his space suit, with his helmet under his arm. Physically he looked better, but she could see from his expression that he knew there was a lot wrong with him. 'My thinking . . . feels kind of slow,' he said.

'It might,' she said. 'But at least you aren't in pain. Are you?'

He shook his head.

'Well, that's something. Sit down. Hi, Del!'

'Robin'll be here in a minute,' Del said, having just appeared from 'nowhere,' suited up and ready to go. 'Hi, Niko, how's it shaking?'

'Shaking is the word,' Laurent said slowly.

'Computer! Virtcall to Charlie Davis. Tell him it's urgent.'

'Working,' said the machine. It said nothing more for some moments.

'Oh, please be home,' Maj muttered. 'You're always home. Almost always.' It was a fair bet, for Charlie studied more than anyone she knew. Maj knew, from talking to a couple of the other Net Force Explorers, that it most probably had a lot to do with his ancient history as a ghetto kid. These days, after having been adopted by a doctor father and a nurse mother, he was relentless in his study of medicine, and—

Light flooded into her workspace. And, oh happy sight, there was Charlie down at his table in his own customary workspace, an old eighteenth-century operating theater with circles of high desks all around it for people to watch while surgeons chopped other people's legs off without anesthesia. The place would have given Maj the shudders if she had not understood it as an expression of Charlie's essentially sardonic sense of humor. 'Charlie!' she cried.

He looked up, slightly surprised. 'I'm glad to see you too,' he said.

She bounded down the stairs to where he sat, nearly

203

tripping as she came down the last couple. 'Charlie,' she said, 'Oh, jeez, I need you, we need you, can you come? Please? Quick!'

He dropped the stylus with which he was scribbling on his desk and got up. 'This a life or death thing?' he said, rather dryly. 'I have a test tomorrow.'

'*Yes!*'

'Oh, well, then,' Charlie said, and immediately followed Maj up the stairs back into her space.

'Charlie, this is Niko. Oh heck, that's not his name, it's Laurent.' They shook hands gravely. 'And that's Del, he's a Net Force Explorer—'

They shook hands too.

'Enough of the courtesies. Laurent,' Maj said, 'has a problem . . .'

She described it in a hurry. Charlie's eyes got wide when he started to realize what kind of thing the microps could do.

'Holy cow,' Del said. 'But what can *we* do?'

'Fight them. Slow them down. Virtually.'

Del looked flabbergasted. Charlie, though, stood very still for a moment, then nodded. 'To chase these things effectively, to interact with them at all, you would have to "map" Laurent's body details – human body details, anyway – onto whatever paradigm you were planning to use for the fighting.'

'*Cluster Rangers*,' Maj said.

Del looked at her, opened his mouth, shut it again. 'Maj,' he said, 'we're simmers, but are we *this* good? Good enough to let someone's life depend on it?'

'If we're not now,' Maj said, 'we'd better get to be, because we have to buy this boy some time. Del, have a little faith in yourself! We've been working with these programming modules for two months now. We're all good at the language.'

'Some of us better than most,' Robin said, walking out of the air, that blue crest of hair nodding jauntily. 'What's the issue?'

'Miss Robin,' Charlie said, with a smile. 'Didn't know *you* were part of this crowd. Changes the tone of the whole affair.'

Robin high-fived him in a cheerful manner as she came over. Maj made a note to pump Robin about where she knew Charlie from, and what was making him grin in that particular way. 'Interesting to see you here, too,' she said. 'Maj, what's the scoop?'

Maj hurriedly told Robin what she needed to know, and what they needed. 'It's an overmap,' Robin said, nodding. 'Not straightforward, but when are they ever? Del, the *Rangers* custom module handler can deal with the details of the overmapping.' She grinned at Laurent. 'For the time being, his body becomes the battleground. But we need a body map to conjoin with the *Cluster Rangers* programming protocols—'

'Just so happens,' Charlie said, 'I have the *New Gray's Virtual Anatomy* in my workspace all the time. That be good enough?'

'What's the resolution?' Robin said.

'Five microns. Ten max.'

'Close enough for jazz,' Del said. '*Rangers* runs at six-micron virtual grain – *Gray's* is a little better than we need.'

'Can you get started on this right away?' Maj said. 'We need to get out of here.'

'We can do better than that,' Robin said. 'We can do it on the fly. I always keep the module manager in my cockpit for fine-tuning the Arbalest simulation in the microsecond pauses.'

Maj's jaw dropped. 'Do you mean to tell me you've been

altering your sim's characteristics *while you're using it?*'

Del, too, was looking amazed. 'I bow to the master,' he said, and put his helmet on. 'If you can do *that*—'

'Hangar's out that way,' Maj said, pointing at the appropriate door, and causing her own suit to appear. 'Laurent, you come along with me again. Charlie, you'd better sort yourself out one of these.'

He blinked, and did so. 'Charlie, you come with me,' Robin said. 'They're all two-seaters. I'll guest you in, and you can sit behind me and give me advice until we've got this solution all properly geeked out.'

They all headed out into the hangars and started the jets warming up. It took a while getting Laurent up into the cockpit – he was slow, and Maj started worrying about exactly how long the effect of being virtual was going to continue to do him any good. But she kept that to herself. 'Maj, ' Del said on 'intersuit radio' as they sealed up the cockpits, 'where exactly were you planning to go hunting these bugs?'

'In *Rangers* space.'

'But Maj, the bad guys know Laurent was there. If we go in there, they'll try to get at him again.'

'Maybe,' Maj said. 'But I'm betting they've already done their worst as far as Laurent is concerned. It doesn't make sense that they'd hold back – he's too important to them. We can't possibly run the modules on my home system, Del! There's not nearly enough processing power! The *Rangers* system has more than enough to spare. And as long as the routines we use to hunt these things through Laurent's body are successfully recast as Rangers plug-in modules, it's all allowable. It should work – we've done enough programming in that system to have a good feel for it.'

Robin looked up from her work in the third cockpit

down. 'There's one other problem, though. If the agents from the other side come in after us—'

'We know this space a whole lot better than they do,' Maj said. 'We have the homefield advantage. They're bound to be scared. I don't imagine that it will go down too well with their bosses if they fail. If I were them, I'd be concentrating on keeping my butt in one piece . . .'

'Ready?' Robin said after a moment. 'I'm still working, but there's no need for us to sit while this is going on. Let's make tracks upward and see where the buggies are hiding.'

'There are your coordinates,' Charlie said from behind Robin. 'The microps have all gone cortical. The program's mapping the sulci now . . .'

'Nebula space,' Robin said. 'The crossmapping is making it equate to the Beehive Nebula, guys . . .'

'Oh, no,' Maj said. That part of space was crawling with the Archon's forces, as well as being thick with a particularly opaque and beautiful, but annoying, nebula. It was a perfect hiding place . . . and a very dangerous place to have a fight, since you could all too easily wind up shooting your buddies.

'The good fight is never easy,' Del said. The hangar finished evacuating – the stars blazed and sang overhead. 'Seven for seven, guys!'

They rose into the unending night. A few minutes later, the synch lasers lanced out, knitting the three ships into a unit. Then the stars' light crashed down on them, pressed them down to nothing and out the other side—

—into glowing cloud, a mass of ion-excited purple, green, and blue, eighteen lighters away. The three of them hung there in silence for a while, looking . . .

. . .and then saw them.

They *were* bugs.

The *Cluster Rangers* game equivalence mapping had taken the projected characteristics of the microps and matched them to the closest creatures in its own 'vernacular.' Now Maj saw what she had quite frankly never cared to see up close – the legendary Substantives, the mindless, nonorganic scavengers left over from 'another space, another time,' remnants of the dark and ancient race with whom the Cluster Rangers' patron species had fought so many long and terrible wars. They were hungry – they ate, and that was all. Many-limbed, many-eyed, nearly immortal, the Substantives lived on energy in whatever form they could find . . . but they best loved the rubble of shattered planets, plenty of which had been left behind, over time, in their dark Masters' wake. Lacking that, they would eat anything – ships, space stations, light, power . . . even dust. That was what they were eating now – using invisible, custom-generated ramscoops to scoop up and devour the glowing dust of excreted parasitic light behind them, the only remnant of their feast.

'*Euuuuuw,*' Robin said softly.

'You got that in one,' Charlie said from behind her. 'That's the myelin sheathing that holds the brain cells together, people, and they're glomming it up like there's no tomorrow. This keeps up for very long, there won't be a tomorrow for one of us.'

Maj was acutely aware of Laurent, behind her, looking out at this with astonishment and horror. 'Let's go get 'em, then,' she said.

The three fighters dove in. Maj, though, was already calculating odds, and beginning to despair. There were at least fifty of these things scattered around that she could see. Substantives had no weapons that she knew of other than brute strength and consuming anything that got in their way – but how representative were these of the true number of microps presently inside Laurent? Were there hundreds? Thousands? Millions? How many more of these were hiding in the nebula?

Del dove in and fired his pumped lasers at one of the Substantives, the closest. It squalled in fury and struck out at him with five or six of those awful clawed legs. 'No effect,' he said. 'Retuning—'

He tuned his lasers further into the blue, came back for another run, tried again. The Substantive lunged at him, just missing with more of those legs. Once again the lasers had no effect.

'Incorrect mapping,' Robin said, as her own Arbalest dove in. 'Going to have to hack at this one, boys and girls. These things are resistant.'

'I thought they might have to be,' Maj said. 'They probably have to cope with white blood cells and such to get their job done.'

'How were these things activated, Maj?' said Robin. 'Net burst?'

'I think so.'

'Huh,' Robin said. 'Well, if we can't destroy them outright, let's try overriding them. They have to accept incoming communication. We may not be able to reprogram them – we don't have the codes for it – but we can try overloading them—'

A moment's pause. Then Robin came around hard and fired at another Substantive.

It stopped scooping up dust, listed over to one side, and began to drift.

'That's it!' Del yelled. 'Come on, guys!'

They went after the Substantives in earnest, hitting

them one after another. One after another, they went down. But more and more of them came out of the nebula. Maj started to worry, for her power conduits were beginning to complain. You could not run an Arbalest forever like this – you had to take it home and fuel it once in a while. And then there was the matter of—

'Uh-oh,' said Robin.

'What?' Maj said, looking all around her. It was a tone of voice she usually only heard from Robin when they were badly outnumbered.

'They're moving again, Maj.'

She looked back, and felt like swearing. One of the Substantives that she had shot up with her retuned cannons was indeed moving, struggling . . . coming back to life. *Are we going to have to shoot all these things up again? We can't! Our own power levels . . .*

Nonetheless she turned around again, wondering how they were going to pull this out without having to go back to base and charge, then come back again. The damage to Laurent's brain would only start all over again. And in the meantime, if the agents from his country should—

'Oh, dear me, no,' Del said.

That was not a tone of voice she cared to hear from Del, either. 'What?'

'Black Arrows, guys,' said Del softly.

Maj looked up in momentary panic, which became more than momentary as she saw the black shapes with their red outlines streaking toward them – five of them. But what the—?

She opened her mouth, closed it again. 'They're not real Arrows!' she said.

'*What?*'

'*Look at how they're moving!*'

Del and Robin were quiet for a moment. Then Robin said, 'They're slow!'

'They're from outside the game,' Maj said. 'They're the agents – the ones that activated the microps in Laurent!'

'And the poor dumb clucks aren't running at multiple G's,' Del crowed. 'They don't know how far the parameters of ships can be pushed in this game. *They don't know the rules!*'

'Then let's not show them right away,' Maj said. 'If they think the normal rules of science obtain here . . .'

She could just hear the others grinning. 'Maj, take point,' Del said, with great relish.

'You're on,' she said, and reached with both arms into the fighting field, the 'glove-box'-like forcefield which the pilot of an Arbalest fighter used to manipulate ship's weapons.

The fight that followed was a sad one . . . for the Arrows.

Maj dove slowly in toward the first of their enemies, watched him react as best as he could . . . then threw her Arbalest around at six gees and cobra'd, letting him pass her, shooting him up from behind. Elsewhere, Del and Robin were using similar tactics. Each took out one of the Arrows, then went for another.

Maj went for her second enemy vessel, diving close. She passed over the other, canopy to canopy, and got a glimpse of the pilot as she twisted away from the Arrow's fire. A woman, she thought – blonde, small. Her helmet hid her eyes, but not her mouth. She was smiling, a look of great enjoyment, and she dove up and around again toward Maj, firing—

I don't like your looks, lady, Maj thought, and clenched her fists in the fighting field. The pumped lasers might

211

have been little good against the Substantives, but they worked just fine against Black Arrows, as the Group had proven the other night. Maj's lasers stitched out from her Arbalest and carved a long line of light and hot metal down the side of the woman agent's Arrow. The blonde's ship tumbled, but she did not know how to handle it – turned, tried to limp away. Maj, though, was in no mood to let it go. She brought the Arbalest around in a turn so tight it would have broken the back of any lesser fighter, 6 G's or better – the blood roared in her ears, but not as loud as her anger. This woman was one of the people who wanted to reduce Laurent's brain to so much strawberry jam, one of the people who had made his young life hell so far, and would have done worse to him and his father for as much of their lives as they had left after they were both dragged home.

Not a chance, lady, Maj thought. This was one of the people who had, even if only for a night, made her turn her home into a fortress, and lock a guest up in the den. Who didn't care who they hurt if it meant getting Laurent, and apparently dead or alive was good enough for this blonde excuse for a human being.

Maj followed her hard, and turned, and turned again, and fired again. The Arrow fled, but Maj pursued – and the Arrow mis-twisted, and Maj found herself sitting, most serendipitously, right on its six.

She fired, and the Arrow blew itself to shreds. Wherever that agent was, in reality, she would not be bothering Laurent again for a little while, anyway. It took some time to get a new ship in this universe.

Maj rejoined the others. Robin was in the act of putting one last agent out of business, blowing his Arrow to smithereens at the end of a long lazy Immelmann turn that was pure insolence in space. A ragged cheer went up from them all at the end of that. But Maj looked with concern up into the cockpit mirror . . . and saw that Laurent had passed out.

'Trouble. We've got to knock those Substantives down again.'

'Can't, Maj!' Robin said. 'No power. Showing red.'

'We have to go back, Maj,' said Del.

'But we *can't!*' Maj said.

'If we don't,' Del said, 'we are genuinely screwed—'

'But Laurent—!'

Then Maj caught the sudden movement. She swore softly and tumbled the Arbalest in y-axis.

—and with no other warning, long slender arrows came lancing past and around them through the darkness of space. Not dark ones, though, not the Archon's ships, but, beyond belief or hope, the white lances of the Cluster Rangers' elite corps, the Pilum Squadrons, every one of them with an odd piece of nose art added – the Net Force insignia. The Pilums' pulsecannon weaponry stitched all the space before them with white lines of irresistible fire, plastering the Substantives with pulsecannon bursts . . . and one after another the giant bugs went limp and still, not moving again.

'The codes have worked,' said one of the Pilum commanders. 'I repeat, the codes work. Squadron, go in and clean them up!'

All those long white shapes disappeared into the cloud. A cheer went up from Maj and Del and Robin and Charlie, and a kind of strangled hoot from Laurent. They all turned tail and made their way up and out of the nebula again—

—and came into clear view of the great arm of the

Galaxy again, the light triumphant against the darkness one more time; and all the stars sang for joy.

One more Pilum came coasting down by them. 'All right, you guys,' said its pilot; and Maj's head snapped up in surprise, for she knew that voice. She peered across the darkness between them, and saw James Winters riding right-hand seat in the Pilum's forward-thrust lance, with a grim grin on his face.

'Captain Winters . . .'

'*Commander* Winters,' he said, 'here, at least. You're done for today, Maj. I relieve you.'

'I stand relieved,' Maj said, and smiled, and slumped back in her seat.

'Now get out of virtual,' he said, 'and for heaven's sake go disarm the alarm system and open the front door, because about eight black-and-whites and a paramedic team from Bethesda are sitting outside waiting for you and Laurent to finish your business here, and your mom and dad are being choppered in and will be there demanding details in about five minutes.'

She had never been so glad to get offline in her life.

It was days before the dust settled. Laurent spent many of them in hospital, having cellular rehab work done on the brain tissue which had been damaged – fortunately, not as much of it as had been feared nor was any of it permanent thanks to Maj's and Net Force's intervention – and having the microps removed. They were a seven-day's wonder at Bethesda, where they were taken for safekeeping until the man who could best manage them arrived.

Maj insisted on being there, at least at a distance. She saw the Swissair spaceplane land at Dulles, and after the cleanup teams got the leftover hydrazine out of the ship, she saw it tugged in to the landing ramp – and she waited with James Winters and her father as the tall blond man with the coat that was too short for his long wrists came up the jetway towards them, having been instructed to bypass immigration. She saw her father and the tall man look at each other . . . and then rush together and hug like a couple of kids. That had been worth seeing.

They had taken him straight to the hospital and left him with the recovering Laurent, with a long story to tell, of which Maj heard at least the highlights. Parts of it, she realized, she was unlikely ever to hear, though her father probably knew about them. All James Winters would say was, 'We have some friends in far places. Sometimes they're in a position to step in and help us. This time was one of those times . . . and we got lucky. They were able to get Laurent's dad away from the security forces just as they took him, and out to where he could phone us the disabling codes for the microps. Not a moment too soon . . .'

Other parts, which she did hear, gave Maj the shivers. 'There's the matter of the agent that Cluj's people sent over to "recover" Laurent,' Winters said. 'Quite a nasty lady – we were glad to catch up with her. There are several incidents which have happened on US soil that we are going to be happy to have the chance to take up with her at last. She'll be here for a while.'

Maj grinned at that. The woman's face had been one of those she disliked at first sight – it was good to know there had been reason for it.

'You thought it through, Maj,' Winters said to her, much later. 'You thought it through, and you followed the hunch when it came to you – and the hunch bought the time that was needed for response by those equipped to respond. You can't do much better than that. I'm proud of you.'

She said nothing, and simply walked along by him, basking in the praise.

'*Now,*' he said, 'we'll talk about why you didn't call me earlier.' And he talked about that, earnestly, for about fifteen minutes, during all of which Maj's ears burned so fiercely that she thought they might set her hair on fire.

Finally, though, her father, walking on the other side of James Winters, spoke up. 'She would probably have called you the night before, Jim,' he said, 'if I hadn't talked her out of it.'

'True?'

'True.'

Winters simply looked at Maj's father and shook his head. Her father shrugged. 'I invoked Occam's Razor,' he said. 'Mea culpa.'

'Mmm,' Winters said. 'Now that you remind me, I seem to remember having put Tabasco in your vodka once.'

'That was *you?*'

Winters nodded. 'Another mistake. So we've made one apiece, now.'

'Can I have that in writing?' said Maj's father. 'And will you give it to my wife? At your earliest convenience.'

The men stood there grinning at one another.

'Where will Laurent and his dad go now?' Maj said after a moment.

Winters sighed. 'It's no surprise we have a protection program for witnesses and other assets,' he said. 'I think we can fairly qualify Armin Darenko as an asset, since he has apparently invented one of the most useful surgical and therapeutic tools of this century. Wouldn't be surprised if he gets the Nobel out of it. That will come later, though. Right now, since he shows no particular interest in returning to his native country – ' and his smile went appropriately wintery – 'we'll "adopt" him and Laurent, find a quiet place for them to settle where they won't be bothered . . . and let them fade into the background.'

Maj smiled. 'New identities . . .'

'I have a feeling your group may acquire a new member,' Winters said, 'with a new name. A couple of your Net Force Explorers associates, of course, are likely to be privy to the information. But I don't think that's going to be a problem.'

'No,' Maj said, 'I don't think so either.'

She smiled, hearing, in the back of her mind, the Galaxy singing; though not nearly as loudly, at the moment, as her pride.

Seven for seven, she thought. *Or nine, or ten . . .*
Whatever!

If you enjoyed this book here is a selection of other bestselling titles from Headline